C000162031

The Secret Sexist

David Bowker was born in Hazel Grove, near Stockport. A former columnist for *New Woman*, he is the author of *The Death Prayer* (soon to be filmed) and *The Butcher of Glastonbury*. He lives in the Bedfordshire countryside with his rightful bride.

The Death Prayer
The Butcher of Glastonbury

DAVID BOWKER

The Secret Sexist

INDIGO

First published in Great Britain 1996
by Victor Gollancz

This Indigo edition published 1997
Indigo is an imprint of the Cassell Group
Wellington House, 125 Strand, London WC2R 0BB

A catalogue record for this book is
available from the British Library.

ISBN 0 575 40054 4

Printed and bound in Great Britain by
Guernsey Press Co. Ltd, Guernsey, Channel Isles

For Jane

'When she appeared for the third time, she was wearing the dress covered with stars, which glittered with every step she took, and her headband and girdle were stars of precious stones. The prince had been waiting some time for her already and pushed his way to her through the crowd. 'Please tell me who you are!' he said. 'I feel as if I had met you already long ago.' Then she stepped up to him and kissed him on the left cheek: and at that moment scales seemed to fall from his eyes, and he recognized his rightful bride.

Jacob and Wilhelm Grimm, translated by David Luke

It was a terrible time to be a man. The very word 'man' had become synonymous with 'bastard'. In those days, you couldn't hold a door open for a woman, even if she looked like a woman, for fear of violent reprisals. It became sexist merely to criticize a daughter of Eve, whereas men (the hairy louts, the insensitive bunglers) were considered fair game.

Real men (that is, those of us who still possessed sexual organs) were forced to go underground. In our hearts we remained hunters and seducers – heart-breaking heroes with rugged jaws and raging hormones – but in daily life we hid our primal urges beneath a tea-cosy of political correctness.

I was so successful in my charade that I actually made a living from it. My monthly column for *Woman of Today* magazine had earned admiring correspondence from women all over the world. I didn't have to lie; I found that if I merely admitted to feeling sad, or insecure, or foolish, in conversation or in print, women automatically assumed that I was trustworthy.

This was how I came to be sitting with my editor, Ariadne Marryat-Legh, at the Grosvenor House Hotel, Park Lane, London, while the British magazine industry handed out cheques to its brightest stars.

I was stuck with Ariadne (fag in mouth, scrawny body drenched in scent derived from the sweat glands of some unfortunate rodent) because Gina, the true love of my life, was at home with stomach-ache. It was always Gina's custom to fall ill whenever she really wanted to go somewhere.

Gina was proud of me, for God's sake, and liked to share in my little victories. This time she had gone to bed with period pains, too ill to drink the vegetable soup I'd heated up for her, and here I was, surrounded by my enemies, with their designer suits and their smug, empty, self-loving faces.

On a neighbouring table, for example, sat Chris Otis Duke, a small man with no chin. Like myself, Chris had been nominated for the Humorous Magazine Writer of the Year award, and he had, in fact, won the award three times in the last four years. To me, his most famous articles, such as 'Why I Hate the Elderly' and 'Dole Queue Spastics', exemplify British journalism at its most sensitive and incisive. His name, incidentally, is an anagram for 'suck this or die'.

To my left, nominated for the more important Serious Magazine Writer of the Year award sat Anne Fermesky, a stout, surly woman of Eastern European origin whose live-in boyfriend gave her regular black eyes. I was disappointed to see that she wasn't sporting a black eye tonight. Anne was renowned for very serious, considered attacks on men and everything they stood for.

Ariadne Marryat-Legh, my mentor and editor, was getting loud and pissed, but as this was the kind of behaviour people expected of her, no one minded.

Ariadne was not a vulgar woman. Rather, she was differently refined. She had been drinking and popping tranquillizers since mid-morning, and not even the thick ochre-coloured mud that covered her face could disguise her ethereal pallor. She was drunker than I'd ever seen her, and although she still barked opinions in my ear like a strident horse, there was something a little lost about her tonight.

I flatter myself that I knew what was hurting her. She had won the Editor of the Year award five times in the past, and yet since 1989 had not once been nominated. She knew, I believe, that her guiding star had not only dipped in its radiant arc but plummeted heavily to earth.

Ask anyone in the media about Ariadne, they will usually say, 'What a marvellous woman! What a superb lady! What a beautiful human being!' She was, in fact, all these things. But Ariadne knew nothing about life or love and had never had a decent orgasm in her life, which was why she was so supremely well equipped to edit a popular women's magazine. (Rearrange the letters of her name, and they spell 'rare hairy meat gland'. Whatever that means.)

On the stage above us stood that top television luminary, Jon Bacon. Although now a late-night chat show host, Bacon had very kindly agreed to hand out awards to us lesser media celebrities in exchange for a large amount of money. Bacon was the kind of chirpy cockney bastard that is popularly believed to have 'personality'. But when he spoke my name, over the surprisingly poor public address system, I must admit that my feelings about Bacon mellowed somewhat. It seemed to me that he even injected a little warmth into his voice as he mentioned me, and I felt, with an unwelcome stab of emotion, that Bacon really respected me. This sudden attack of mawkishness was not helped by the cheers and applause my name provoked from my fellow diners. These loathsome slugs actually *liked* me, and I was touched by their good taste.

Ariadne's hand was now resting, presumptuously but forgivably, on my leg. And as that gorgeous star of stage and screen, the tall, the ever-posh Julia Courtney, mounted the stage to open the sealed envelope and read the winner's name, my editor gave my leg a supportive squeeze. With the dazzling smile that has endeared her to millions, Julia opened the proffered envelope like one who would rather spend her spare time promoting worthy causes. Then she made the announcement.

'And the winner is . . . Guy B. Lockheart.' That, by the way, is my name.

There was a tremendous whoop from Ariadne, who had already claimed this moment as a personal victory, and then, feeling foolish, vulnerable, heroically shy, I tottered up on to the podium like a man who is about to receive a cheque for fifteen thousand pounds.

I received a crappy award from Jon Bacon, in the shape of a silver quill stuck in an ink pot, and a cheque from the lovely Julia. It was Julia that I was most interested in, but when she leaned forward to kiss me, she kissed the air like a member of the royal family, rather than sticking her tongue down my throat as the occasion clearly demanded.

Julia Courtney and I have a lot in common. Like me, she was born on 1 May. I once nearly went out with a girl who once nearly went skiing with her. None the less I could see, even in my unexpected euphoria, that Julia had never read my column and hadn't the faintest idea who I was.

Bacon guided me to the microphone. In view of the fact that I had been voted Humorous Magazine Writer of the Year, he was probably hoping that I would say something funny to liven up what was proving to be a very dull evening.

And indeed, in the unlikely event that my colleagues should see fit to honour me, I had prepared a short speech. It went something like this: 'I don't believe in awards, and you're all wankers.' Alas, choked by emotion as I was, I could only say, 'Thank you. This is a real surprise. Thank you all.'

Through an adrenalin-charged haze, I glimpsed Chris Duke flirting with his footballer boyfriend, not interested in me at all, and Ms Fermesky staring at me coldly, clapping in a slow, calculatedly mocking manner.

I returned to my seat, close to tears, and Ariadne sprayed me with cold champagne, not the cheap stuff this time, but

Bollinger RD. It tasted so bitter to me, after that evening's excessive tippling, that it might as well have been fizzy urine.

People I'd never met before reached forward to pat my shoulder and shake my hand and Ariadne, observing my emotion, went into mother-mode and drowned me with affection and pretty cooing noises.

I realized then that I was just like everyone else. The deep repugnance I had always felt for prizes had been based, largely, on the fact that I'd never won any. Suddenly, I felt like one of those sobbing beauty queens whose hobbies include swimming, meeting people and working for world peace. How strange it was to think that a lump had been brought to my throat by all these hacks when, ten minutes earlier, I would have paid good money to see them being machine-gunned to death by a maniac in a burger bar.

Soon Anne Fermesky was up on stage, receiving a bigger cheque than I as Serious Magazine Writer of the Year, but, happily, not being cheered as loudly. Nobody liked Anne, least of all Anne. She shook her cheque for twenty thousand pounds in the air as she bellowed, 'This is for all the anorexic women who have been murdered by the slimming industry.' It wasn't, of course. It was for Anne Fermesky. She was going to spend twenty thousand pounds on cream cakes.

But in my present beatitude, I could not even condemn my harshest critic, who once, at a conference about pornography, publicly referred to me as 'that glib fuck'. So I applauded Anne, because life had already punished her enough by making her small and fat and shrill when she had always wanted to be beautiful and loved.

I was getting happily drunk when a member of the aristocracy came on stage. She was a small, elegant woman with neatly coiffeured grey-blonde hair and bright, fiercely intelligent eyes. She was called Lady Philipa Bowden and was well known for her exhaustive work for charity. She was probably a good friend of Julia Courtney. This evening, Lady Bowden was here to talk about something called the Ellen Quirke Memorial award. Lady Bowden acted as patron for the Ellen Quirke Trust.

Ellen Quirke had been a devout feminist who had risen to fame in the late sixties. She was an early contributor to *Woman of Today*, in the daring days when black models were occasionally featured on the magazine's cover. She and Ariadne had worn bell-bottoms and head bands and spent long nights smoking dope and wishing they could have saved Janis Joplin. Ellen had become one of Britain's leading lesbian thinkers, before her premature death in a knife fight with someone who was trying to steal her girlfriend.

'This award,' Lady Bowden was saying in her clear, crisp voice, 'is awarded annually to the writer working in the British Isles who has contributed most in the past twelve months to understanding between the sexes . . .'

I suddenly became aware of a sharp discomfort in my bladder. I arose, intending to visit the little boys' room, but immediately Ariadne snatched at my arm and pulled me down. She was hissing at me with some urgency.

'Guy, for God's sake!'

Bridling, I said, 'Ariadne, I'm dying for a slash.'

But she hushed me quickly, almost quivering with indignation. I rose and she snatched at my arm again. A peculiar tug-of-war broke out between me and this gaunt, elegant woman and I noticed that people were beginning to stare. Even the icily composed Lady Bowden was showing signs of interest. Then I noticed chirpy Jon Bacon signalling to me frantically from the wings. By earnestly pressing down the air with the palms of his hands, he was indicating that I should, at all costs, remain seated.

Then, as in a dream, I heard Lady Philipa say the following: '"I have never understood why women are treated as second-class citizens. All my life, women have

14

impressed and amazed me with their wisdom, their grace and their immense capacity for compassion."'

Which women did she have in mind, I wondered? Margaret Thatcher? Myra Hindley? Imelda Marcos? Then breathlessness overtook me as I recognized the origin of this prose. Lady Bowden was quoting from one of my own articles.

'"Whatever her shape, her height, her weight or her colour, I unreservedly accept the female of the species as my friend and tutor. I hope that my fellow men will do the same. And boys, we'd better not skip school, because we have an awful lot to learn."'

Simultaneously, the women in the audience applauded wildly. The men sat motionless, confused and mildly nauseated, until their wives, girlfriends and mistresses bullied them, with glares and nudges, into constrained spasmodic clapping. Only Anne Fermesky refused to clap. Only she refused to respond to the bland garbage that had made my reputation. I have to admit that, all things considered, I'm with Anne.

Lady Bowden was giving me an impressive build-up. 'Allow me to quote,' she said, 'from one of *Woman of Today*'s correspondents, who writes: "I extend my heartfelt thanks to your magazine for restoring my faith in men. Thank you for giving me, each month, a man with a heart, a brain and a soul. Thank you for a man who makes me laugh and cry, and who I and readers like me have come to think of as an ally, a brother and a friend. Thank you, thank you for Guy B. Lockheart."'

Applause. Then, with poise and perfect timing, Lady Bowden said, 'Ladies and gentlemen, the winner of this year's Ellen Quirke Memorial award is Guy B. Lockheart.'

Hence I was honoured for the second time that evening. I renegotiated the stage, and the women present cheered me without restraint. I shook hands with Lady Bowden, who

15

was not so much clapping as patting an imaginary hamster. But she stopped patting long enough to hand me an envelope and a bronze statuette in the shape of a fat woman.

'Well done,' she said, grinning at me with surprisingly yellow teeth. Given her background, you'd have thought she'd have known how to use a toothbrush.

Intellectually, I was disgusted with the Ellen Quirke Trust for giving me their award, and with myself for accepting it. But emotionally I was overwhelmed. As I approached the microphone, I began to weep. Naturally, the women in the audience loved this. Quite a lot of them began to weep in sympathy with me. However, I'm quite certain that most of the men present would have liked, at that moment, to dry my tears with an acetylene torch.

'I wasn't expecting this,' I sniffed. 'I am very surprised. But I must admit to feeling like a fraud as I stand here tonight.'

The hall went silent. I had their attention.

'I don't really deserve this award,' I continued, boyishly wiping my streaming cheeks on the sleeve of my tuxedo. 'I feel that people should receive awards for making an effort of some kind. Whereas I have earned this award by making very little effort. All that my work involves, after all, is loving women. And I have always found women very easy to love. Thank you.'

The girls loved this, and their menfolk pretended to love it, snarling at me through clenched teeth. Perhaps they were simply jealous. Or perhaps they sensed that I was not a new man at all, but one of their own kind.

And so it came to pass that on this warm August night I reached the pinnacle of the journalistic profession, which, on the scale of human achievement, placed me only slightly above pimps, executioners and workers in the nuclear power industry. That was my reward for thirty years of lies and hypocrisy. That was what my life had become.

16

Part One
Secrets

The First Secret

I spent the night in Ariadne's spare room. She lived in a mews cottage in South Kensington that was the size of two bus shelters stacked vertically. I was awoken at about six by the sound of Ariadne barking like a dog in her sleep. At least, I hope she was asleep.

There had been a party after the awards ceremony. I don't remember much about it, apart from a drunken conversation with Chris Duke, during which I told him, to my eternal shame, that I had always admired his work. I have the nightmarish feeling that he, in turn, lavished praise on me. This is the way I behave when I'm truly intoxicated. I engage in mindless niceness, and then awake with my temples pounding and the taste of someone else's bottom in my mouth.

As my vision came into focus I saw something shining on the dressing table at the end of the bed. It was the Ellen Quirke Memorial award, and my heart sank, because I knew that it weighed a fucking ton and I'd have to carry it home with me. Hastily, I arose, showered and dressed. Then I threw my clothes and my statuette-in-the-shape-of-a-fat-woman into my overnight bag and went downstairs to the kitchen. As rapidly as possible, I made some tea and ate a bowl of muesli.

There was a reason for my haste. Ariadne lived alone, and, apart from a rather large spider that lodged behind her drinks cabinet, I was her only guest. I'd stayed with Ariadne once before and had received the strong impression that she'd been waiting for me to 'take her'. During my visit she had wandered around her tiny abode in a loose dressing gown, coughing constantly, blowing smoke out of her cavernous nostrils and calling me dreadful pet-names like 'doll' and 'cutie', as if I was Tony Curtis dressed as a woman in *Some Like It Hot* and she was the horny little bell boy.

Had she caught me that morning, I knew that in addition to the above, I would have been in for a leisurely reflection on her friendship with the late Ellen Quirke and how people like me were carrying on Quirke's work now that Ellen, all sixteen stone of her, was keeping the ivy green in Highgate Cemetery.

As I was writing a friendly note for Ariadne, I heard her moving about overhead. I did not delay. Quicker than the time it takes to say 'vaginal discharge', I snatched up my belongings and hurried out into the noise and glare of the city.

Gina was waiting for me at Stockport station. I'd phoned from Euston to tell her when to expect me. I also informed her that she was married to a 'lucky winner'. I was leaning out of a window as the train approached the station, and I saw her standing on the platform in the distance, staring into space. As the train coasted towards her, I waved as if I was in a film: a war hero, decorated with the ribbons of valour, returning home to his sweetheart. But she didn't see me, and instead looked completely the wrong way – if Gina had been in a film, it wouldn't have been the kind of film in which lovers recognize each other across crowded stations; it would have been a film where people walk into walls and fall over and mistake window cleaners for presidents.

When I stepped down from the train, she saw me and ran towards me. You could tell she'd been ill. Her face was absolutely ashen, and her short dark hair was stuck up on one side, as if she'd just got out of bed. I dropped my bag and we threw our arms around each other, right there in the middle of the platform, and I could sense other passengers cursing inwardly because a loving couple were standing in their way.

'How do you feel?' I asked her.

'Shit,' she said. 'Shit, but happy.'

'Me too,' I said, kissing her.

'Come on, then. What do they look like?' she asked me.

'What do what look like?'

'The award thingies.'

'They're in my bag.'

'Show me, show me!'

'Not now. Later, Gina. They're right at the bottom.'

'Aw, let's have a look.'

'No. They're right at the bottom.'

'OK. But what do they look like?'

'Well, funnily enough, the cheque for fifteen thousand quid looks like a cheque. For fifteen thousand quid.' She whooped with delight. 'It came with some kind of sculpture that looks like a piece of shit.'

Her face lit up. 'Really? It really looks like a piece of shit?'

'No. It looks like a quill stuck in a fucking ink pot. But the Ellen Quirke thing doesn't come with any money, unfortunately. It's just a statue shaped like an overweight lady.'

(It was all right to use words like 'overweight' and 'lady' in front of Gina, because she was certain enough of my feminist credentials to know that I only used such terms ironically.)

We left the platform and began to walk down the steps. 'I didn't realize before, but we've got one of Ellen Quirke's books,' she said. She corrected herself: 'You've got one of her books – *The Life of a Woman*.'

'Close,' I said. 'It's called *A Woman's Life*.'

'What's it about?'

I paused before answering. I hadn't read Ellen Quirke's book and suspected that no one else, living or dead, had read it either. It was one of those books, like *Ulysses* or *A Suitable Boy*, that you turn to out of a sense of duty but are forced to abandon after page fifteen because you can't work out what's going on and, what's more, don't fucking care. But I didn't want to appear shallow, especially in front of someone who respected my opinion, so I said, 'Well, it's basically an autobiographical novel about a woman who grows up feeling doubly alienated, first of all for being a woman, and secondly for being a lesbian.'

'Yeah. I know,' she said. 'It tells you that on the cover.'

Caught out, I turned the tables on her. 'Why just read the cover, Gina? Try reading a whole book, for once . . .'

She laughed and hit me. We were quiet as we walked out to the car-park. It was about two-thirty in the afternoon. The sun was beating down on the tarmac. 'What will it lead to, do you think?' she wondered, as we entered our white mini and sat in its smouldering seats, she at the wheel.

'Where will what lead to?'

'The fact that you've won things. What difference will it make to *us*?'

She meant, 'Will people give us money?' We had never had enough money, and at that time of our lives a change in our financial circumstances was the only kind of change that would have seemed significant to us.

I sighed.

'Well, darling one,' I said, 'I don't know for sure. But maybe more people will know who I am now. I'm not just a prick any more. I'm an award-winning prick. I suppose I could always capitalize on my near-fame by having another stab at writing that book.'

For years I'd been planning a serious treatise on how middle-class men have never really accepted feminism,

22

merely learned to employ politically correct language and behaviour in order to attain sexist ends. The working title for this book was *The Secret Sexist*. It was a boring idea and I knew that if I didn't find a suitably boring publisher for it soon, its topicality would be lost, because this was 1994, and educated people were already growing weary of sexual politics. People still *pretended* to give a toss, but soon they would stop pretending, and men and women would revert to viewing each other as, at best, worth a shag but utterly beyond redemption.

'But, Guy, how would you go about researching a book like that?' said Gina, frowning slightly as she unintentionally sped through a set of red traffic lights. 'It's a nice idea . . . don't get me wrong . . . but who on earth could you talk to? Where *are* all these "secret sexists"? I mean, I'm sure they exist, but I've never actually met one.'

I maintained an undignified silence.

We lived together, Gina and Natalie and me. Natalie was Gina's kid sister. We lived in a comfortable detached house in Hazel Grove, Cheshire. I'd married Gina four years before, when Natalie had been eighteen. Their mother had been alive then. But now it was just me, and two dark sisters who liked having a 'new man' about the house. It was a home that had known tragedy, but I was happy there, writing my shitty articles, surrounded by music and girlish laughter and Tampax bloody tampons. The number of the house, for those who like omens, was thirteen. A real house, in a quiet suburban road called Shepley Drive.

When we returned home, Natalie leaned out of her bedroom window and dropped rose petals on our heads as we approached the front door. Natalie had also made a cake and iced it. Gina had written MY GUY across the surface of the cake with Smarties. I knew that the Smarties were Gina's doing because they were all wonky. Everything that

Gina did came out looking wonky. Her wonkiness was one of the things that had first attracted me to her.

When we walked into the kitchen, Natalie came up to me and punched me in the stomach affectionately. 'Well done,' she said, 'you clever bastard.'

Gina threw her arms around me. 'He *is* a clever bastard, isn't he?' she echoed. Natalie, taking the lead from her sister, threw her arms around me also, so that I was soon completely smothered by love and admiration. In those days this happened to me every single day of my life.

Despite feeling half-dead, Gina insisted on making a pudding for this celebratory meal we were about to have. Natalie and I tried to persuade her not to bother, because she was unwell and, besides, we already had the cake. But we only succeeded in annoying her. Gina seemed to think we were implying that she was a lousy cook, and that a dessert prepared by her was likely to give us all food poisoning. Feeling an argument looming, Natalie and I vacated the kitchen and left her to it.

Natalie went upstairs to take a shower, and asked me to talk to her while she did so. I'd been 'talking to' Natalie while she showered since she was fifteen years old.

I watched, too. But I was always careful not to watch too closely, lest I be mistaken for one of those unsavoury brutes who like looking at beautiful naked women. So whenever Natalie was in the shower and I was sitting in the chair at the end of the bath with a grandstand view of the entire proceedings, I always made sure I had a magazine in my lap. I've found that browsing through a magazine on such occasions helps to convey an impression of relaxed, non-predatory detachment.

Today's publication was a magazine for feminist men called *Achilles' Heel*, and on its cover was the legend 'Guy

Lockheart on Men Who Can't Show Affection'. I read the said article aloud to Natalie, glancing up regularly to note her reactions and to slyly monitor the soap's progress.

This is what I read: 'As a child, I was taught that it was wrong for boys to kiss each other. My brother Ben, two years my senior, was taught the same thing. Unfortunately, he found me irresistible and when I started school at the age of four, he kept running up to me in the playground to smother me with kisses. I complained to my parents, who sternly took Ben aside to warn him that *little boys don't kiss little boys*.'

Natalie stopped me. 'What? Is that true?'

'Afraid so.'

'Your brother Ben, Ben the macho man, used to kiss you?'

'Frequently. And, indeed, passionately.'

'And your parents told him he couldn't? Guy, that's terrible.'

She soaped her pubic hair into an impressive lather, and I disguised my interest by pretending to study a squashed fly on the shower curtain. 'He should have been Italian,' I said, with visible regret. 'He could have snogged me as much as he'd liked, then.'

'He should have been *my* son,' she said indignantly. 'I'd *never* have punished him for showing love.'

She washed her non-existent breasts for the second time, and I saw her long dark nipples stand to attention. I quickly switched my gaze to her eyes, saw amusement there, and knew that she knew that I'd been looking. Furthermore, she knew that I knew that she knew.

Dry-mouthed, a little desperate, I said, 'How's the violin practice going?'

She didn't answer, merely looked down and smiled in a secretive way. I realized that she was staring at my lap. Without my noticing, my copy of *Achilles' Heel* had fallen to the floor and there was now nothing to shield my crotch from Natalie's gaze. She could see that I had a huge throbbing bulge in my trousers.

The celebratory meal was a happy affair, although Gina could eat very little of it, because she was allergic to so many foods. Natalie could eat what she liked, but Gina was allergic to most things, including life.

Our dinner was washed down with a bottle of Australian sparkling wine that was so good it almost made me like Australians. Unfortunately Natalie insisted on playing her new CD on the stereo: the soundtrack of some shitty film about a woman who plays the piano all the time. It was the kind of film that cultured people aren't supposed to laugh at. The film's heroine can't speak, so she uses the piano to express her innermost soul, only all it sounds like is someone going *plink-fucking-plonk* on a fucking piano. After a while, I complained.

'Natalie, are you planning to play this dreadful shite all night?'

To my surprise, Natalie did not take offence. 'No,' she said sweetly, rising from the table. 'I'm not. Tell me what you want to listen to, Guy, and I'll put it on.'

Gina, her mouth full of pudding, said, 'No, Nat. We can't just let him have his own way all the time . . .'

'Tonight we can. This is Guy's meal, in Guy's honour.' She bowed to me theatrically from the CD rack. 'So, Guy, what would you rather hear?'

I didn't really want to hear anything. So, manfully, I relented. I insisted that Natalie keep her shitty CD on, and we listened to it as the candles burned low and the vast, sad house made its presence felt all around us. After a while, Natalie gave Gina a conspiratorial smile and said, 'Will you ask him now?'

Gina glanced at me, lowered her eyes and giggled. 'No. *You* ask him.'

Natalie also giggled and the two sisters began to wrestle half-heartedly. 'Cheat! You said *you'd* do it . . .'

'I've changed my mind.'

This rather puerile exchange went on for some time.

'Ask me what?' I demanded. 'What are you laughing for?'

There was another interval of girlish tittering. Gina took possession of herself long enough to say, somewhat breathlessly, 'We've got something to ask you. Or rather, Natalie has.'

Natalie collapsed into fits of hysterical laughter. Between shrieks, she succeeded in saying, 'No. You ask him.'

'Oh, fucking forget it.' I sighed. I arose and started to clear away the dishes.

My sudden show of activity shocked them into sobriety.

'No, sit down,' said Natalie earnestly.

'Sit down, Guy,' echoed Gina. 'It's important.'

'If it's so important, why are you laughing?'

'It's embarrassing as well as important,' Gina assured me, gently taking my arm.

'What?' I said. 'Like the Labour Party?'

'Don't try to be clever,' urged Gina. 'Natalie wants to ask you something.'

I looked at Natalie, who was holding her hand over her mouth and turning very red in the face. I'd never seen her like this before. 'No, she doesn't,' I retorted. 'She's trying not to laugh.'

But I was sufficiently intrigued to allow Gina to ease me down into my chair. I waited until Natalie had wiped the tears of mirth away from her eyes with a paper napkin. Then she said, 'We're both very fond of you, Guy.'

'Oh. Thanks,' I said.

'Even if you *are* a grumpy grouch,' added Gina, pinching

my cheek. This was so like her. Only Gina and her idol, Cliff Richard, could use an expression like 'grumpy grouch' without dying of shame.

'Well?' I said. 'What's all this about?'

Right on cue, Gina said, 'It's about babies.'

'Yeah,' said Natalie. 'I want to have a baby, Guy.'

I failed to see what any of this had to do with me. 'Well, why don't you get a boyfriend? I've heard that having sex can help women in your situation.'

'It isn't funny,' warned Gina.

'It can be,' I replied. 'It depends who you're having sex with.' They were not amused, so I said, 'Anyway, if it isn't funny, why were you both pissing yourselves a minute ago?'

'Because this isn't easy to talk about,' explained Gina patiently. 'And you're not exactly helping.'

'All I said was, "why can't she get a boyfriend?"'

It seemed like a reasonable enough question to me. Natalie was twenty-two years old, and had been celibate for more than a year. It was a political celibacy, brought about by her involvement in a society called SMASH (Serious Musicians against Sexual Harassment). After fucking boys on a casual basis for years, she had reached the conclusion that they were lousy lovers, as well as oppressors of women, children and animals. And fish. She was not interested in sex with women, so she had decided that her body should belong to no one but Natalie. Her avowed desire to become a mummy had therefore come as something of a surprise to me.

'There are ways of getting pregnant without having sex,' said Natalie pointedly.

'You shouldn't believe everything you read in the New Testament,' I said wittily, but to zero applause.

There followed a pause that could itself have been described as pregnant. But not particularly silent. That shitty

28

soundtrack from New Zealand was still playing. In retrospect, it now seems fairly obvious where my conversation with Gina and Natalie was leading, but at the time I didn't have a clue what was coming. So I felt as if I'd been hit over the head with a blue whale's testicle when Gina suddenly said, 'Actually, Guy we were rather hoping that *you'd* help Natalie get pregnant.'

'*What?* What did you say?'

Natalie smiled sweetly. 'It's all right. I'm not planning on raping you or anything. I just thought that, well, if you'd got any sperm going spare, you might, you know, bear me in mind.'

To tell the truth, I'd been shedding my spare sperm with Natalie in mind for years. But I knew I couldn't say this, so I acted all flustered and said, 'Fuck. I don't know. I don't know, Nat. It sounds like a bit of a weird idea to me.'

Gina moved her chair closer to mine and clasped my hand. 'I know, I know. It seemed weird to me at first. But listen, listen. Natalie and I have thought this through very carefully. She wants a baby. But she doesn't want a relationship. So what does she do? She turns to a nice man, i.e. you, who, well . . .'

Natalie took over: 'Who isn't chauvinistic or aggressive, and who wouldn't dictate to me about what I could or couldn't do with my child. *Our* child. A man who really respects women. Guy, how many men have I known who fit that description, do you think? Come on. How many?'

'Besides me and Nietzsche? None.'

'Exactly,' said Natalie.

'That's right,' agreed Gina. 'One of Natalie's main problems with men is that she's seen how good our relationship is, and has never been able to settle for less than her big sister has got.'

'And why the fuck should I?' demanded Natalie.

'Exactly! Why the heck should she?' said Gina, misquoting her sister on purpose, as only a true Cliff Richard fan could.

Natalie took up the gauntlet, and proceeded to ram it down my throat. 'And the fact that we all live together makes it all sort of neat, don't you think? All right, perhaps it might seem a bit odd that you're married to my sister, and yet I'm the one who wants your baby. But the truth is, Gina doesn't feel the need for children yet and I *do*. I want a baby so much that it's hurting me, Guy.'

I looked at Gina, who confirmed her sister's hurt with a suitably heart-rending nod of the head. (God, women should be ashamed of themselves. They really should.) Then Natalie took my other hand, so that I was now truly their wide-eyed prisoner.

'Natalie's worked it all out,' said Gina. 'You know how regular her periods are . . .'

'Yeah. She gets them every month,' I quipped, also to no applause.

'Every twenty-eight days, to be exact,' corrected serious Natalie.

'And that means we've been able to work out when she ovulates,' continued Gina. 'Which is next Tuesday. That'll be day fourteen of her cycle. But to be on the safe side, you'd better donate your sperm from Sunday, right through till Thursday . . .'

'What?' I said. 'Non-stop?'

This *did* make them laugh. They seemed to relax a little. Natalie poured more wine into her glass and my own. 'All you have to do is come into a glass for me. I'll take the glass away and do the rest.'

'Well, it'd better be bigger than *that* one,' I said, pointing at my wine glass. 'In fact, I'll probably need a pint pot.'

They laughed again, and I felt my penis straining against the zip of my jeans. Natalie had given me a thrill by saying 'come into a glass for me'. But as much as their idiotic scheme appealed to me, it occurred to me that I might be giving in too easily, so I frowned pensively and said, 'Er, hang on a minute, women. I'm not quite sure about this, you know.'

Natalie sagged as if she'd had a puncture. Neither her face nor her body moved, but something, a certain *spiritus*, drained out of her. And I saw plainly, for the first time, how much motherhood meant to her.

'It's good that we can joke about it,' I said, doing a passable imitation of a responsible adult. 'But let's remember that we're talking about making a new person here. Not a novelty, a little doll for us all to play with. A living, breathing person, with real feelings and needs . . .'

Gina squeezed my hand. 'Guy, do you think we haven't already discussed this?'

'Well, you haven't discussed it with *me*. Why wasn't I in on the discussions? It seems to me that I'm a pretty crucial part of the fucking plan . . .'

Gina sighed. 'Guy, we were afraid to ask you.'

'Afraid?' I repeated, reminding myself unpleasantly of a character in a play by Harold Pinter.

In a tired voice Natalie said, 'We were afraid you'd say no.'

I looked at her, saw that a single artistic tear was gliding down her face. That tear gave me quite a jolt. This was a woman who seldom showed emotion. 'Hey,' I said. 'Hey.' I reached out and wiped her face with the back of my hand.

Gina got up, circumnavigated the table and cradled her sister's head against her midriff. 'Don't be sad, Nat. Guy hasn't said he won't do it.' She looked at me, seeking reassurance. 'You haven't said you won't do it, have you, Guy?'

'No,' I said. A pause. 'I haven't said I *will* do it, either.'

A flight of fresh tears escaped from Natalie's eyes. Gina held her sister closer, making hushing noises and regarding me with barely concealed hostility. I decided that my token show of resistance had gone on for long enough.

'No, no,' I blurted. 'It's all right . . . Forget everything I've said. I'll do it.'

'What?' said Gina. 'Say that again.'

'I'll do it. Why not? We all love each other, don't we?'

They whooped and laughed and descended on me, until I was covered in salt water and smothered with love. They didn't seem to realize that their proposal had launched me into a state of intense sexual excitement. They actually believed I was being selfless. Even as they pressed their soft faces against mine, I remember thinking, *How? How could they not know?*

I couldn't sleep that night. I'd entered a state of near panic. Adrenalin was buzzing through me like a virus. Every time I closed my eyes I saw an image of Natalie, floating darkly, holding a small baby-sized bundle to her breast and smiling like an unblessed virgin.

I got out of bed and wandered, naked, out to the bathroom in the dark. As I pissed, still in the dark, I saw my reflection in the mirror. I looked as pale as a vampire, only not as interesting. Then I went downstairs to the living room and turned on the light.

I walked over to the book-case and carried out an experiment in bibliomancy, opening books at random in the hope that the immortal gods would advise me about Natalie. The first book I selected was Voltaire's *Candide*, which I opened on page twenty-nine to read: 'But how could such a beautiful cause produce so hideous an effect upon you?'

I found this slightly worrying, so turned to *The Highway Code* and saw: 'If anything falls from your vehicle, stop as soon as you can with safety and remove it from the carriageway.' Next, I opened *The Blue Peter Annual* and read the words, 'Hello, there!'

But the most impressive lines by far came from *The Woman in White*: 'I should never, perhaps, have heard even the name of the woman who has lived in all my thoughts, who has possessed herself of all my energies, who has become the one guiding influence that now directs the purpose of my life . . .'

The Second Secret

I'd been in love with Natalie for a long time.

Almost as long, in fact, as I'd been in love with her sister. It's popularly believed that it's impossible to love two people at the same time, but, in truth, it's incredibly easy. It's just impossible to tell the truth to both of them at the same time. Or either of them, at any time.

When I first met Gina, I was a postman. *Her* postman, to be exact. I'd just been thrown out of art school, and dumped by my girlfriend. I was living with my parents and leading a fairly ghastly existence. Every morning I delivered mail to one of the best neighbourhoods in Hazel Grove, and I was always getting crushes on the women on my round. I wasn't alone in this, believe me. There are an awful lot of sad bastards working for the Royal Mail.

There was a girl called Donna Sturmey, who lived on Denison Road, and there was Gina Kemp, who lived round the corner on Shepley Drive. I also quite fancied Gina's mum, because she used to come to the door in her dressing gown, joking with me as she thrust out her large operatic breasts. She had the kind of cleavage that can induce vertigo.

One Valentine's Day, I sent an anonymous card to both Donna and Gina, deciding that if I passed either of them in the street, I'd ask them how they liked their cards. I never saw Donna Sturmey again. Perhaps my card had encouraged her to leave the country. But I passed Gina every week for the next two months. She was usually walking to the woods, and she always seemed to look right through me, as if I didn't exist. Finally, I stopped her and asked her why she kept giving me dirty looks. Apologetically, she explained that she hadn't been giving me looks of any kind. She couldn't even see me. She was short-sighted, but too vain to wear her glasses. And when I thought she'd been looking right through me, she'd actually been trying to work out whether I was a person or a lamp-post.

I asked her out for a drink, right there and then. She put on her glasses to see what I looked like, and after some consideration said, 'Yes.' It was all pretty easy after that. She laughed at my jokes and I laughed at her Cliff Richard records. She was beautiful, and gawky, and a little old-fashioned. We were meant to be together.

Gina was quite an original. She claimed to be a Christian, but didn't believe in God. This amused me. She believed in the Son of God, but not God Himself. To me, this was like believing in Mickey Mouse, but not Walt Disney.

She lived with her mother, Rose, and her fifteen-year-old sister. Despite their four-year age difference, Natalie and Gina looked more like twins than sisters: they were both long, thin and dark. They each had identical tiny moles above their upper lips, which gave them the appearance of French courtesans at the court of the Sun King. But their bodies were inhabited by very different spirits. Gina was awkward, sweet and diffident; she was perpetually acquiring ugly bruises by walking into furniture. Natalie was insolent and self-assured: if she didn't feel like talking, she'd simply sit and stare you out for the hell of it.

When I first met Gina, she was a virgin. Seven long months were to pass before she admitted me to her bed. But I quickly discovered that her virginity, her quasi-Christianity and her questionable taste in popular music were not indicative of her general character. She was no prude, and delighted in the copious cusses that tripped from my foul tongue. She also, from the first week of our kissing acquaintance, shocked me to the bone by wandering about in front of me, stark labia naked.

It wasn't just Gina, for Pan's sake. All the women in that household behaved as if nudity was the most natural state in the world. I was allowed to look, but not touch. Imagine the strain that this placed on my wrist.

They left their soiled laundry everywhere. I could have made a fortune by exporting their dirty knickers to the Middle East. They urinated with the lavatory door wide open, like innocent chattering children. They discussed their periods with me, asked me to fetch their sanitary towels from the bathroom cupboard. Rose had taught her daughters to have no shame.

Which brings me to George Kemp, absent husband and father. I am forgetting my journalistic training. A newspaper editor once told me that the basic principles of reportage are: 'Who? What? When? Where? Why?' To which I am tempted to reply, 'Bollock, Bollocked, Bollock-Time, Bollock-Land and who the fuck cares?'

But, for the record, George Kemp was a keen amateur yachtsman who, in 1980, had been keen and amateurish enough to take to the waves at Torbay, in spite of a gale warning. The boat sank, taking George with it, and his family had never recovered from their delight.

When he was alive, or at least not dead, Kemp had been a martinet, a bully of women and children. He used to scream abuse at Rose when his coffee was too hot to drink. He forbade the children to make noise in his presence, and banned the colour pink from the house. Kemp believed that pink things excited negative human emotions. If he accidentally chanced on a pink bar of soap in the bathroom, he would shriek and stamp his feet, thereby proving his own theory. His doctor referred him to a specialist, who concluded that Kemp had a rare condition known as Knapp's disease, which meant, for all practical purposes, that he was a mad bastard who didn't like pink.

But Kemp had his uses. He had been an economist, fanatical about profit and loss, with the emphasis on profit. His savings and shrewd investments had left his family well provided for. All that the women who survived him required was his absence. And so a house that had once resounded to high-pitched shrieks and the stamping of patriarchal feet came to be filled with music, laughter and sweet womanly ease.

The Kemps were a musical family. Gina was a classical pianist, and sister Natalie played the violin. Gina had won many prizes in her early teens, but by the time we met, her confidence had faltered. She'd recently flunked her audition for the Royal Northern College of Music, simply by playing notes in her Bach recital that Bach disclaimed all responsibility for. 'Technically, I'm really good,' she said. 'But I don't have any confidence.' This meant that she could play the piano brilliantly, as long as no one was listening.

Rose ran an antique shop in nearby Bramhall village, not because she needed to, but because it amused her. She drank to excess and appeared to thrive on it, her naturally sanguine temperament enhanced by a bottle of Chardonnay or a tumbler of iced gin. When pissed, her filthy raucous laughter could drown the sound of passing aircraft. She was fascinated by witchcraft and occultism. Arcane amulets, inscribed with runes and sigils, dangled in her Death Valley cleavage.

She was hugely energetic, and cooked elaborate banquets, just for the hell of it. She often said that I was like a son to her, but when she was tipsy and casually groped my arse, I wondered what kind of son she had in mind. The name Rose was too small for her. She should have been called Diana Isis Lilith Demeter Om. Or Dildo for short.

When Gina and I had been going out together for about a year, I resigned from my position at the Royal Mail. This upset my parents, who threatened to throw me out on to the street. Rose, who took the view that I was meant for greater things than bending birthday cards and being chased by snapping poodles, invited me to come and live at her house.

I accepted her offer, and moved my clothes, records and books in with me. Among the books was a set of feminist classics that my ex-girlfriend had forced on me, in a vain attempt to raise my consciousness. There were titles by De Beauvoir and Gloria Steinem, and that lesbian with glasses and white hair, whose name I can never remember. Also present were the works of Ellen Quirke, as well as a book by the then-unheard-of Anne Fermesky called *Sister be Fat, Sister be Proud*.

Rose and Gina were extremely impressed to see these volumes in my possession. Not that they had read them themselves, or had any intention of doing so. Until I came along, the most radical publication in their home was *Woman of Today*. But like most middle-class women, they thought of themselves as feminists, and liked the idea of living with an enlightened man. The fact that I could wash dishes and make macaroni cheese augmented my saintly image. It didn't take much. Good manners and a few unread books were enough to launch me upon my career as a professional liar.

From an early age, Natalie was destined to be the true feminist of the family. By the age of fifteen, she had already fucked enough boys to know that she didn't like them much. She never looked the part; it was Gina who had the floppy sweaters, the boots and sexy dyke haircut. Natalie's hair was always long, straight and flowing, making her resemble the High Priestess from her mother's tarot pack. She also wore dresses, make-up and pretty girly hats. She had a real disdain for men, and an ardent desire to be separate from them. But she couldn't be separate from me; not just because I lived with her, but because she was so close to Gina. So I became her token male: a subject for analysis, experiment and occasional ridicule.

Once, Natalie came home from a rehearsal of the Bramhall Youth Orchestra and walked in on Gina and me while we were lying in bed together. She must have been about sixteen. For a laugh, Gina pulled down the duvet so that her kid sister could have a good look at my inert cock. Laughing merrily, Natalie proceeded to prod my organ with the tip of her forefinger, just to see if she could make it go hard. Lo and behold, she succeeded. Meanwhile, Gina lay contentedly by my side, amiably pointing out interesting facets of my florid member to her sister. They reminded me of two nurses having a sly laugh about the body of a dead or unconscious patient.

I suppose that this incident sounds like a lie: one of those fabricated letters from a porn magazine. But the porn version would end with me 'shafting them both senseless, then withdrawing my throbbing prick to shoot gallons of thick white come-juice all over their naked breasts'.

In reality, I simply lay there, fully erect but powerless, knowing that I was expected to remain docile and passive until the amused spectators got bored and my poor teased penis wilted. Yes, I was being interfered with, but it was only happening because Gina and Natalie trusted me. Good God, it was worse than that. They thought I was *harmless*.

My first ever attempt at journalism was a trite little piece called 'Why Men Can't Cry in Public'. I'd been looking through Gina's women's magazines, and had come to the conclusion that the articles in them would be fairly easy to invent; they were always full of anecdotal ramblings and fictitious 'friends' who supplied relevant quotes at key moments. To a born liar like myself, no problem at all.

I'd spent years on the dole. I thought it was about time I made an effort of some description. So, with Gina's encouragement, I wrote fifteen hundred words of shit. Gina typed them out for me, and I sent the result off to *Woman of Today*.

To my surprise, a deputy editor called Melissa Benz-Frobisher rang me up a few days later and said she liked my writing, even if my choice of subject matter was a little hackneyed. 'Tearful men have been done to death, really. But we've been looking for someone honest and funny to write about penises for us. I mean, how does it feel, as a man, to have this silly little thing hanging down between your legs? It must be awful.'

Without a moment's hesitation, I agreed to debase myself for *Woman of Today*'s readers and my fate was sealed. Under normal circumstances, Gina and Natalie would have been delighted for me. I was about to write for the only magazine they read. But this was November 1989, and they had other things to think about.

Rose's drinking had been getting out of control. A man she'd been having an on-off affair with for years had died in the summer, rapidly turning her from a cheery wine-lover into a raging alcoholic. She became moody and argumentative, and started passing out in unlikely places.

On 2 December, Natalie's seventeenth birthday, Rose crashed the car into the garage door and entered the house reeling, complaining that she couldn't see clearly. We thought she was just blind drunk.

She was admitted to hospital for a series of tests that proved inconclusive. I clearly remember the last time we visited her. We took her a box of Lindt Chocolate Kittens, a bottle of Perrier water, some magazines and a bag of satsumas. She'd been in hospital for two days, and still couldn't see properly. She was wearing an awful orange nylon night-dress that didn't belong to her, because she'd spilt soup on her own. The orange night-dress was the kind of garment that hospitals inherit when poor people die, and that are then washed and lent to other poor people.

Gina kept saying that her mother looked better, and Natalie and I agreed. It wasn't true, though. Rose looked terrible. Her skin had turned an awful shade of yellow ochre and the bones of her face were protruding ominously.

Suddenly Natalie said, 'Wanna hear a joke, Mum?'

Rose looked surprised. Natalie never told jokes. But Natalie told her joke anyway. It was the one that goes: What do you call ten thousand men lying dead at the bottom of the sea? Answer: Not enough.

Rose considered this witticism for a moment, then sat up in bed and opened her mouth wide. We thought she was about to laugh. Instead, she vomited dark blood all over the counterpane. Weeping, Gina grabbed a paper tissue and dabbed ineffectually at her mother's face, while Natalie ran to get a nurse. But Rose was already dead. Her liver had literally exploded. It was the worst thing I'd ever seen.

I never *did* like that joke.

The Third Secret

I heard Natalie say, 'Is that it?' Then I heard Gina laughing. When Gina was really amused, she shrieked like a jungle sound-effect in a Tarzan film. That was the noise she was making now.

Natalie spoke again. She sounded half-amused, half-scathing. It was a tone I knew well. 'I mean, what the fuck am I supposed to do with *that*?'

Offended, but trying not to show it, I emerged from the bathroom, zipping up my trousers. Gina and Natalie were on the landing, outside the door to Natalie's bedroom. Natalie was wearing a tiny white T-shirt and no knickers. A fine line of pretty dark hairs stretched from her pubic hair to her navel. They were a hairy pair, these sisters. They had hirsute thighs and armpits long before Anne Fermesky published her second feminist classic, *Sister be Brave, Don't Have a Shave*.

'All right,' I said. 'What's the big joke?'

Natalie didn't answer, merely raised the glass she was holding to the level of her chin and peered at its contents with a supercilious smirk on her handsome face. Something told me she was not impressed.

'What happened, Guy?' asked Gina.

'What do you mean?' I said, knowing full well what she meant.

Natalie said, 'She means, "Is this really your sperm or did you pay a fucking pygmy shrew to spunk up on your behalf?"'

I regarded the small watery-grey squirt that was resting forlornly at the bottom of the glass. My first semen donation for Natalie was little more than a dribble and bore scant resemblance to the 'gallons of thick white come-juice' that I ejaculated in my unreconstructed fantasies.

Natalie said, 'I've been reading about sperm quality. Did you know that the quality of the sperm you produce now depends on your life-style three months ago?' She held the glass up to the light. 'What were you doing three months ago, Guy? Hitting yourself in the balls with a mallet?'

'I'm sorry,' I said gloomily. 'I don't know what's the matter with me. I usually produce about ten times that amount. Don't I, Gina?'

I had rather hoped that my wife would take this opportunity to offer her support. Instead, she burst out laughing. Women can be heartless bitches at times like this. I'm not making excuses, but it was Gina's fault that I produced such a pathetic amount of semen in the first place.

To have a really good wank, one needs to relax and focus all one's attention upon a filthy image or idea. So at the appointed hour of seven p.m., while the sisters waited in Natalie's bedroom, I locked myself in the bathroom and tried to imagine being fucked by Natalie.

I sat on the linen basket with my trousers down, cock-in-hand, striving to visualize this vulgar vignette, but whenever I came close to getting an erection, Gina knocked on the bathroom door and said ,'Pstt! Have you done it yet?'

I don't know why, but she interrupted me three times. Perhaps she knew what I was trying to imagine, and wanted to stop me before things got out of hand. Eventually, I opened the door and told her to bugger off. She offered to speed things along by giving me a hand-job. By this stage, I was willing to try anything, so I let her into the bathroom and she took over.

And that explains why I had such an uninspired orgasm.

How can a man enjoy a wank when his wife is not only watching, but doing his wanking for him?

Disheartened, I went out to see my brother. Ben lived in a small house on Old Mill Lane with his wife Rachel and their two small children. Ben looked like a young Burt Reynolds. Rachel was a gentle blonde with eyebrows like Mariel Hemingway and the shy, slow grace of a sister-of-mercy. She was a sweet Catholic girl who had disappointed her family and the Holy Father by climbing into bed with my tattooed heathen brother.

I had a cup of tea with them while Rachel fed the baby and Ben bounced his two-year-old son on his lap. The boy was named Sam Francis, after Sam Cooke, Ben's favourite male vocalist and Francis of Assisi, Rachel's favourite saint. The eight-month-old girl on Rachel's lap had been christened Kate Mary, after Kate Bush, Ben's favourite female vocalist, and Mary, Rachel's favourite virgin.

'I liked your new article,' Rachel told me.

'What was it about?' I enquired.

'Er, something about men who don't like women, I think. It was very good, anyway.'

'A heap of festering dog-shit,' scoffed Ben. I knew he hadn't seen my latest column. He was merely making an educated guess, based upon his knowledge of my past achievements.

'Ben, don't swear in front of the children,' admonished Rachel, turning to me and smiling.

'Eh?' protested Ben, who could never let anything go. 'Dog-shit isn't swearing. It's a whatchacallit. A proper English noun. I shit, you shit, the dog shits.'

'*Ben!*'

Rachel admired me, and Ben resented the fact, mainly because everyone knew what a journalist was, and he only did some kind of printing job that was too boring to talk about. Even his own wife wasn't sure what he did. Sometimes, if he was in a communicative mood, he'd try to explain. He'd use phrases like 'ink sprocket' and 'computerized press gauge' and everyone's eyes would glaze over with boredom, and then he'd give up.

'Gina must be proud of you,' said Rachel.

'Yes,' I said. 'She's my number one fan.'

'Oh, fuck off!' groaned Ben. 'Please. Just fuck *off*!'

Ben and I climbed into his clapped-out third-hand petrol-gobbling Mercedes and went out for a drink. This was a regular ritual for us. Every fortnight or so, we'd go out for a drink to remind ourselves that we had absolutely nothing in common.

We drove to a hotel in Disley that was famous for adultery. We sat in the bar and watched a smug white-haired man buying drinks for a fat-legged woman in her thirties. Ben and I guessed that he was her boss, and she his secretary, although she probably insisted on being described as a 'personal assistant'.

'Yeah,' sneered Ben. 'I'll bet she's about to "personally assist" him out of his extra-large string underpants.'

There was a lull in the conversation. This always happened when Ben and I got together. To be honest, there was generally more lull than conversation. It seemed pointless to sit there, feeling bored, when I had something interesting to say, so I told Ben what I'd agreed to do for Natalie. I was slightly taken aback by the vehemence of his reaction.

'You dozy get!' he spluttered.

'Why? What's the big deal?'

'You can't do that. What about Gina?'

'Gina knows. It was Gina's idea in the first place.'

'Jesus-on-a-stick! I thought she had more sense.'

Ben had always been very fond of Gina, and the feeling was mutual. He had always regarded Natalie, on the other hand, as a 'miserable stuck-up bitch'. And he strongly

45

disapproved of the idea of his brother engaging in human reproduction with someone who didn't laugh at his jokes.

'What if she runs off with the kid?'

'What do you mean?'

'When it's born, she might run off with it. She might never let you see it.'

'That's not going to happen. But even if it did, I wouldn't care. I don't want a baby. Not yet, anyway. It's Nat who wants the baby. I'm just helping.'

'Oh, fuck! You stupid, stupid twat. Get me another pint.'

I went to the bar. When I returned, Ben had his next question prepared. 'And are you telling me that Gina just sits back and watches while you shag her sister?'

I tutted. 'I don't shag her. You daft sod. We're using artificial insemination.'

This silenced him for a moment. He calmed down slightly. I realized that most of his outrage had been based on the misconception that I was having sex with two women, while he had to content himself with one.

'So what happens?' he asked. 'Do you wank through a key-hole or what?'

'I come into a glass. Then she takes the spunk away, fills a plastic syringe with it and squirts it up herself.'

Ben looked disgusted. 'The dirty cow!'

There was a pause. White hair and fat legs got up to leave. We watched until they were out of sight, then Ben said, 'What are you going to tell Mum and Dad?'

'I'm not about to tell them anything. And neither are you.'

'Won't they think it's a bit funny when Natalie starts walking around with a beach ball up her fucking jumper?'

'Yeah. But they won't know who the father is, will they? Unless you tell them.'

He gave a non-committal grunt. This made me nervous.

'Ben, don't you *dare* tell them. They'll never understand in a million years.'

'They're not alone.' He threw back his head belligerently and swallowed half his beer. 'Fuck! She's a silly bitch, that one. Why can't she just go out and poke someone. Anyone! She could shag a tramp.'

'She doesn't like men.'

'Ah. I see. That's why she likes you, then, is it?' He stared at me mournfully. 'Oh, Guy. Don't do it. Please.'

'Ben, it's not a big deal.'

'Don't tell me that. A kid's a huge fucking deal. You fuck up things for Gina, mate, and I'll never forgive you. I think the world of that girl.'

'Gina doesn't mind, Ben. Why won't you listen?'

'Don't do it. Please.'

My brother's appeals made no difference. The next night, Monday, I kept my tryst with that rather unattractive glass. This time, I tried to help myself along by creating a little *ambiance*. I asked Natalie and Gina to stay downstairs, out of the way. On no account, I insisted, were they to disturb me. Then I borrowed a pair of Natalie's knickers from her room, stripped naked and lay on my bed with the knickers over my face.

They were a fetching pair of briefs: pale blue silk, with dainty white frills. They had also been recently laundered; I wouldn't want you to think I was a pervert or anything. But they still carried a faint scent of her: a smell like a cool wind blowing through a field at harvest time.

For that night and the remainder of the week, those knickers served me well. My subsequent semen output was well up to standard and the sisters declared themselves happy with my efforts. By Friday, when this, the first ever 'National Spunk Week' had come to an end, I knew it

47

would have been sensible to return Natalie's drawers to Natalie's drawer. But I found, touchingly, that I'd grown emotionally attached to her fragrant briefs. So I hid them in the inner pocket of the dark suit I wore for funerals, reasoning that Gina wouldn't go near anything that reminded her of death.

One week passed. The sisters grew more and more excited, eagerly anticipating the date of Natalie's next period. Natalie insisted that she didn't *feel* pregnant but, as Gina and I pointed out, how could she possibly know what 'pregnant' felt like?

Natalie's period was due on a Tuesday. On the day before, she and Gina went out to Boots to buy a pregnancy-testing kit. Tempting providence, they also purchased and refrigerated a bottle of that sparkling wine that makes Australians seem likeable.

All Tuesday, they waited.

Natalie did not bleed. This was very unusual for her. Gina's periods were all over the place (if you'll pardon the expression), but Natalie was a twenty-eight-day marvel. Gina could barely contain herself. She kept running up to Natalie and kissing her. 'You're pregnant, Nat. I know you are. I *know* it.'

And each time, Natalie would shake her head and smile her secret smile.

That night, before we went to bed, we all hugged each other and agreed to meet in the bathroom at eight in the morning, where we would learn whether the Goddess of Love and Sorrow had granted Natalie's deepest wish.

'Ready . . . aim . . . fire!' yelled Gina.

Natalie was squatting on the lavatory, holding a white strip of plastic in the line of fire while she had a wee. Gina was peering between Natalie's legs to make sure she was doing it right. The instructions referred to the white strip of plastic as an 'hCG indicator'. I didn't know what 'hCG' stood for, but from where I was standing, it may as well have been 'hairy cunted girl'.

When the device was suitably drenched, Natalie took it out and laid it on a saucer. The instructions said that you were meant to wait for three minutes. Natalie and Gina waited. I went on to the landing, trying to look impartial. I wasn't nervous, merely curious. Eventually, I heard Gina say, in a strangely neutral voice, 'It's blue.'

I walked back into the bathroom to find the sisters staring at each other in amazement. I didn't know what blue meant. I said, 'Is blue good or bad?'

Natalie's eyes were shining. 'Blue's fucking brilliant.'

'She's pregnant,' said Gina. I could see that she was really stunned.

None of us knew what to say. Gina hugged Natalie, and I hugged Gina. Then I hugged Natalie, who, implausibly, had my baby inside her. Natalie was actually shaking as she put her arms around me.

Then I surprised myself by doing something that no self-respecting new man should ever do. I started whooping and beating on my chest with both fists. 'Man!' I cried. 'Fertile! Ooh! Ooh! Ooh!'

Natalie and Gina laughed delightedly. They thought that they were witnessing a clever parody of phallocentric pride. What they didn't realize was that my exuberance was sincere and spontaneous. I couldn't help myself. Next to God, I owned the most magical bollocks in creation.

'Pregnant!' I crowed. 'All it took was a glass! I'll bet the fucking glass is pregnant, too!' I pounded my chest again. The blows hurt, but the pain felt right. 'Man! Virile! Ooh! Ooh! Ooh!'

On the following Sunday afternoon I attended a meeting of my men's group. We always met on the first Sunday of every month, taking turns to visit each other's homes. Besides me, there were four other men in the group. The oldest member was Charles, a rather dissolute and *soigné* TV director who appeared to have no real interest in feminism or male bonding but was fond of making vulgar remarks. He was forty-one.

Then there was Gordon Wright, a 29-year-old solicitor who was only slightly less complacent than Charles, but had earned our lasting respect by having an exceptionally large penis, which we only found out about by accident. One afternoon, after a sweaty game of five-a-side, the rest of the group and I had joined Gordon in the shower, and there it was – this great bloated primeval sausage that swung from side to side when he moved. We were all rather sick at heart when we first beheld this awesome trunk, especially when we looked down and compared it to what little we had to offer. But the fact that Gordon owned such an instrument, yet had never once boasted about it, led us to conclude that he was a humane and decent man.

Our most troubled member was Malcolm Bowers, a small, geekish individual with over-active armpits. Malcolm had spent most of his thirty-four years feeling guilty because of what men had done to women, and frustrated because of what women had never done to him. Malcolm's strongest ally in the group was Vaughan, thirty-seven, a bearded psychotherapist who had an irritating tendency to ruin perfectly satisfactory conversations with idiotic quotations from various American self-help manuals. But despite their earnestness, they were both likeable men, and, had they not been present, Charles and I would only have cracked feeble jokes and encouraged Gordon to talk about his penis.

In terms of group politics, I was somewhere in the middle, being neither as serious-minded as Malcolm and Vaughan, or as genially apathetic as Gordon and Charles. That is, half of me wanted to be honest and enlightened, while the other half thought that feminism really stank. The advantage of being in the group was that I could openly admit to such crass prejudices, and not be condemned. For we observed the rule that everything said during meetings was to be treated in the strictest confidence, and that candour was to be respected above all other considerations, including tact, political correctness, and good taste.

This month, it was Malcolm's turn to play the hostess. We seated ourselves on cushions in the living room of his unattractive flat. He lived above a toy shop in Marple, and had made a small apartment seem even smaller by painting its entire contents brown. At the beginning of each session, it was our custom to summarize recent events in our lives for the benefit of our fellow group members. This month, Malcolm was sporting a black eye. Dolefully, he told us why.

'As you know, I care deeply about the issue of pornography and feel bitter because of what pornography says about the way men perceive women.'

'Yes,' interrupted Charles. 'But do you *like* porn?'

Every month, whenever Malcolm raised the topic of pornography, Charles asked this same question. 'You ask me that question every month, Charles,' said Malcolm wearily.

'And I'll keep asking it, dear boy, until I get a straight answer.'

For a few seconds, Malcolm opened and closed his mouth like a goldfish. Then, as if he thought he was being quick-witted, he said, 'And what about you, Charles? Do *you* like pornography?'

'Yes, I do, Malcolm. I bloody well love it. How about you?'

Malcolm looked most unhappy. I couldn't help feeling sorry for him. In his position most people would have lied, said anything to win the argument. Not Malcolm. He was determined to tell the truth, no matter how wet or foolish it made him look. 'Well, pornography excites me sexually. But I wouldn't say I liked it.'

There was a silence, while Charles smiled wistfully, apparently satisfied with this reply. Malcolm resumed his story. 'Anyway, as part of my plan to co-ordinate an anti-pornography initiative in Marple, I decided to picket a local newsagent that sells pornographic magazines.'

I was amazed. 'How does one picket a newsagent?'

'Well, first of all, I asked the shopkeeper to remove all the pornographic magazines from his shelves. He refused. So I stood outside, and whenever I saw a customer approach the door, I asked them to boycott the shop because it sold pornography, and pornography degrades women.'

Vaughan said, 'Did anyone listen to you?'

Ruefully, Malcolm shook his head. 'I think they thought I was mad.'

Charles laughed delightedly. 'And what did the shop-keeper think?'

'He thought I was mad, as well. He came out and threatened me. When I refused to move, he hit me in the face, and that's why I've got a black eye. He was Asian, too. I didn't know that Asians hit people. Yes, Gordon. I'm glad you think it's funny . . .'

Gordon had been trying so hard to contain his mirth that his face had turned purple. On hearing Malcolm's accu-sation, he let out a great shriek of girlish glee. The rest of us, with the exception of Malcolm, joined in.

Seeing that Malcolm was upset, Vaughan said, 'Come on, Mal. You must admit there's a funny side to what you've just told us . . .'

Malcolm would admit no such thing. Vaughan suggested that we create a wall of love around Malcolm.

'Not another one,' grumbled Charles uncharitably. He had a point. Every month, when Malcolm was crying or looked close to tears, the rest of us ended up hugging him to show our brotherly solidarity. The trouble was that hugging Malcolm always made him more upset. This afternoon was no exception. We crawled over the brown carpet to embrace Malcolm, forming a nest of entwined bodies. In no time at all, we were all holding our breath and he was sobbing piteously.

Afterwards, as always, he thanked us. 'I want to say that this last year has been a very difficult time for me, in that I've been breaking up from my partner, and the break-up has been long and painful. I honestly think this group has saved my life. No. I mean it. Thank you, everyone. Thanks for all your love and support.'

We told him not to mention it.

It was my turn to speak next. Because of holidays and illness, six weeks had passed since our last meeting. An awful lot of semen had passed into the glass since then. Calmly, without elaboration or fancy adjectives, I told the group about my involvement in Natalie's pregnancy. Slowly, their facial expressions changed from polite boredom to envy.

'You lucky bugger!' said Charles.

'Why is Guy "lucky", Charles?' challenged Vaughan.

'You mean you don't know?'

'I mean that you seem to be implying that his situation involves some kind of macho victory. And I want to know why.'

Charles lit a cigarette and coolly blew the smoke in Vaughan's non-smoking direction. 'You're quite right, Vaughan. The thought of getting a twenty-two-year-old up the spout *does* seem like a victory to me. Probably because I'm twice her fucking age. So, yes, I think Guy's a very lucky bugger.'

'But, hang on,' pointed out Gordon. 'He only used artificial insemination.'

'I don't care if he sent his spunk down the channel fucking tunnel. It's a triumph for the male gender, mate.'

'That's just the way you feel, though,' said Malcolm. 'Guy doesn't feel that way, do you Guy?'

After a long pause, I said, 'No. I'm afraid that Charles is right. The thought of Natalie having my baby appeals to all my worst instincts. There's something I think you should all know. Something I haven't been honest about in the past.'

I paused. My mouth was dry. They stared at me expectantly. 'But I've got to talk about this, because it's driving me fucking mad . . . I love my wife. You know that. She's the best friend I've ever had. But I don't lust after her, and I never really did. Natalie's the one who gives me a hard-on.'

Malcolm was shocked. 'Guy! That is *so* sexist! I can't believe you just said that.'

Gordon gave one of his rare displays of animation. 'Judgemental! Malcolm's being judgemental! That's totally against group policy.'

Vaughan echoed this viewpoint. 'As you always say yourself, Mal, we're here to be honest, not to sit in judgement.'

Feeling humble, Malcolm apologized to the group. He said, 'You've made me feel humble. I apologize to the group.'

I continued, 'I suppose you all think I should tell Gina what I've just told you?'

'Yes. I think you should,' said Malcolm.

'Malcolm!' snapped Gordon.

'Sorry,' said Malcolm.

'Have any of you come acoss a book called *I Love You If You Love Me?*' asked Vaughan, knowing full well that none of us had. 'No? You should read it. It makes a very interesting distinction between "positive and negative truth". Meaning that complete honesty in relationships is bound to be hurtful. And that sparing your partner a truth that can only hurt them is not deceit or cowardice, but a sign of genuine love.'

'Sounds like bollocks to me,' commented Charles.

'Yes, Charles. Well, it *would* sound like bollocks to you.'

'So who thinks I should tell my wife that I fancy her sister?' No one reacted. 'Come on. I'm *inviting* you to judge me.'

Only Malcolm thought I should tell Gina. 'What worries me, you see, is that your attitude to your sister-in-law . . .'

'Natalie.'

'Yes. I'm sorry to say this, Guy, but I find your attitude to Natalie deeply sexist. You're obviously pleased with yourself because you've helped her to conceive . . .'

'He gave her his spunk,' said Charles. 'Why can't you come right out and say it?'

Flinching slightly, Malcolm resumed, 'But your pleasure at her conception has nothing to do with respect for her needs as a woman. All you seem to be saying is that you find her attractive, and therefore relish the thought of having your issue inside her.'

'Issue?' scoffed Charles. 'Issue? What is she? A fucking magazine rack?'

I said, 'Well, Mal, it's like this. I'm not going to tell my wife what I've told you, because I know it'd only hurt her. In fact, it'd shatter her whole conception of who I am. She thinks I'm above mere lechery. So does Natalie, for that matter.'

'In other words,' said Malcolm sadly, 'you've been living a lie.'

The Fourth Secret

For the next few months, Gina and Natalie were deliriously happy. Natalie's Professor Emeritus at the Royal Northern College of Music had allowed her to take a year out. She would now start her final year in the following autumn. Consequently, she had time on her hands, which meant time to piss about with Gina.

After my initial euphoria, my spirits had slumped a little. I'd remembered that I didn't particularly like children. I admitted this to Gina, who said 'That's other people's children. You're bound to feel differently about your own.'

'What if I don't?' I retorted. 'What if I like my own children even less than other people's?'

She kissed me indulgently. 'You're too sensitive. Don't worry. It'll be Natalie's baby. It won't really belong to you.'

A fair point. Yet Gina clearly thought that the baby was going to belong to *her*. She and her sister had already started choosing names, nine months too early. Gina brought home a book of wallpaper designs, with the intention of turning the spare bedroom into a nursery. My role in the proceedings was over. I didn't count. I was just the good sower who, having sowed his seed on fertile ground, was expected to gather up his seed-bag and fuck off.

I didn't mind being excluded from their baby games, mainly because it was so good to see Gina happy and motivated again. Since her mother's death, she had come to view life as a high-risk commodity, unworthy of serious investment. While Natalie had been studying at the Royal

Northern College of Music, leading the kind of arty existence that should rightfully have been shared by her elder sister, Gina had all but given up music, and allowed herself to sink into apathy. I'd tried everything to inspire her, including marriage. Nothing had worked.

But for a while, it seemed as if what had happened to Natalie had restored Gina's faith in that God she didn't believe in.

All that winter, while the mother-to-be hovered between ecstasy and nausea, I churned out my shitty articles. The Award-Shaped-Like-a-Piece-of-Shit had resulted in a spate of commissions. I wrote about 'Men Who Do It With Their Socks On', 'Men Who Are Afraid of Sex', 'Women Who Fake in Bed' and even 'Women Who Fart in Bed'. The only article I didn't write was 'Are Women Really as Thick as Women's Magazines Would Have Us Believe?'

I appeared on television, late at night on BBC2 when absolutely nobody was watching, talking to journalists I hated and who hated me about subjects we knew nothing about. They were supposed to be live discussions, but they were recorded earlier in the day, in case someone like me said a word like 'fuck' and the viewers complained. I realized that I was only there at all because I was cheap, and the producers of these programmes had low budgets, which meant that they couldn't afford to make the boring programmes they really wanted to make. I also noticed that although the producers and the presenters and most of the other guests of these late-night schedule-fillers hated each other, they still socialized and went to each other's weddings and threw up in the toilets at the Groucho club together. Whereas I knew nobody, and at the end of the evening, while they were climbing into the same taxi, I was always left alone, with nowhere to go but my hotel room. That should have told me something.

Ariadne was still my number one fan, and, because she

was vain, she imagined that everyone in the media read her magazine, and were therefore aware of me and my award-winning column. She failed to grasp that other editors only read their own magazines, and were far too preoccupied with their own exclusives and sales figures to care about hers. Or that members of the public bought magazines to while away the time while they had a shit, and didn't give a toss who had written the articles they read, or, in fact, didn't realize that articles were written by anyone.

Yes, people had heard of me. But only the kind of people who knew the name of the editor of *Guardian Women*. Real people, people who mattered, didn't have a clue who I was. I was just one of those boring arseholes who put on their best suits to talk about books on BBC2, late at night. The kind of person whose very face makes viewers turn to their partners and say, 'Nothing on the telly.'

I had no illusions about myself. I'd won a couple of awards because I'd been slightly original in a field of activity where most people were absolutely useless. That was all. But to Ariadne, who had discovered me, I embodied living proof that her judgement was flawless, her taste divine.

Before Christmas I travelled to London to meet her for lunch. We dined on the top floor of L'Escargot, away from the people who wanted to be seen. I'd barely stabbed my avocado before she announced, 'I've got a proposition for you.'

'Oh, yeah? What?' I asked nervously, as I pictured her freckled bosom bearing down on me.

'It's about this novel you want to write.'

'What novel?'

'You know. *The Sexy Secret*.'

'*The Secret Sexist*,' I corrected her. 'And it's not a novel. It's meant to be a . . .'

'Not a novel?' she snapped, her nostrils flaring. Ariadne

couldn't bear to be contradicted. 'It's *got* to be a novel, kid. You want people to buy it, don't you?'

I nodded.

'Right. This is what we do, then. You write a novel, full of that lovely sweet warmth you put into everything ... good characters ... a lovely, sensitive book. And I print it in instalments, chapter by chapter, a *Woman of Today* exclusive. Yes? Before any lousy publisher gets a sniff of it. Whadya say?'

'Well, I, yes ...'

'It'll be great for you. Everybody's serializing books nowadays. You'll be following in the tradition of Charles Dickens ... Thomas Hardy.'

'Melvyn Bragg,' I added.

'Don't get too ambitious,' she cautioned. 'But we'll do it properly, with a real contract and everything.'

'The only trouble is, I've never written fiction,' I objected. Then I remembered that I had never written anything *but* fiction. 'But I'll think about it.'

She poured more wine into my glass, slopping some of it over the crisp white linen table-cloth. 'You'd be *mad* to say no, Guy. I mean it. Really *bloody* mad.' (She silently mouthed the word 'bloody' just as elderly northern women mouth words like 'period' and 'hysterectomy'.) 'But I want the truth, remember. Our readers are sharp cookies. They're not easily fooled. So no fibbing. I want you to write about men. Not men as women see them, or men as they want to be seen, but men as they really are.'

For a second or two, I thought she was serious. Then she said, 'But nothing too unsympathetic, please. The characters can be as sexist as you like, as long as they're *nice*.'

I sighed, without meaning to. 'What about swearing?'

'If you must. But no more than one "fuck" a chapter.'

'What about words like "cunt"?'

She grimaced and shivered, as if she'd swallowed a bad oyster. 'Ugh, no. That is *such* an ugly word. I won't have it in the magazine.'

She suggested that I submit a couple of chapters and an outline. She also said that I could take as long as I liked, as long as I took no longer than three months. Then she reached into her Liberty shoulder-bag to extract a paperback, which she thrust aggressively across the table at me. The book was by someone with the unlikely name of Professor Dudley Fingerman. Its title was *How to Write*.

'And before you start,' she said calmly, 'it might be a good idea if you read this.'

On the train home I found myself wedged into a corner by a trio of female fabric designers who had visited a London design fair. They were all drinking cans of lager and bitching about their male employers. Every so often they flashed me a friendly smile, but had I been their colleague, they'd have been ripping the piss out of me, too.

I was attempting to read Professor Dudley Fingerman, but the noise made concentration difficult. Chapter One was called: 'Why Write at All?' Dudley said:

> Some people write for pleasure. Others write for financial gain. Whatever their motives, all budding writers need to know what it is they want to say. Otherwise, *why write at all?*

Having read this, I turned back to the preface, where there were a few words about Dudley himself. To my surprise, there was no mention of him being mentally handicapped.

The woman next to me said, 'Did you see the way Edgar was holding in his stomach?'

'Yeah,' said one of her friends. 'And did you notice that

the more he held in his stomach, the more his bum stuck out?'

Observations like this were enough to make the rude girls roll about, roaring with uncontrollable laughter. They kept this up until Stoke-on-Trent. And when one of them reached into her bag and extracted a copy of *Woman of Today*, I knew that it was time for me to leave.

I wandered down the corridor in the direction of the buffet, pursued by their sniggers. I bought some crisps and a coke from the buffet, and leant against the wall in what I hoped was a devil-may-care manner. A fattish guy in a business suit joined the queue for the buffet. As he waited, I felt him staring at me fixedly. I was just about to move away when he said, 'Is that you, Girly?'

I flinched. Nobody had called me 'Girly' since school. That had been my nickname: they started by calling me Guy, then Guy Fawkes, then Girl Guide, before finally settling on Girly. There had been no malice behind it: I went to a grammar school, where it was considered stylish to have an insulting name. One of the most popular boys in the school, Rob Blower, was known as 'Fart-pants'. We also had a 'Turd', a 'Quim', a 'Snotty' and even a 'Twat-face.' But the man in the business suit had been known to everyone, teachers included, as 'Bomber'. His real name was John Lancaster, and, until my late teens, he had been my best friend.

'Bomber?' I said. 'Is that you?'

His round face creased into a smile, and he relinquished his place in the queue to give me a spirited bear hug. 'Hiya, mate!' he said. 'Great to see ya!'

I said, 'You're looking prosperous.' It was a stupid thing to say: a line that I'd heard estranged uncles use on each other when they met at Silver Wedding anniversaries. Something that old men resort to when they can no longer bring themselves to say, 'You're looking good,' or even, 'You're looking well.' But Bomber didn't seem aware of my social blunder. In fact, he swaggered a little, as if I'd paid him a great compliment.

'Can't say the same for you, Girly,' he sighed, looking down at my blue jeans as if they were smeared with excrement. 'Still on the dole, I see.' He laughed throatily. 'Only joking. Here, let me buy you a drink . . .'

I resisted, but he bought me a Scotch anyway. 'Where are you sitting?' he asked me.

I jerked my thumb in the direction of second class, which British Rail now insisted on calling 'standard' to disguise the fact that it was really third class. 'Come and sit with me,' said Bomber. 'I'm in first.'

'I haven't got a first-class ticket,' I protested.

'Don't worry about it,' said Bomber, slapping me on the shoulder so boisterously that I banged my head against the wall of the carriage. 'If the ticket fella comes round again, I'll do the talking.'

He'd been the same as a child. Bomber used to believe that he could 'fix' anything. He was usually right. He'd been a rich kid, alway's owning the newest, most expensive toys before anyone else in the neighbourhood. He used to have smoked salmon for tea, while I was eating egg and chips. My farts only ever used to smell like his on Christmas day.

The first-class compartment was virtually empty, apart from a prim-looking woman across the aisle who was aiming her pointed nose at a copy of *Country Life*. 'Anyway, what are you doing with yourself, these days?' queried Bomber.

'I'm a journalist,' I said. 'Magazines.'

'Yeah? We both lie for a living, then.' He laughed again. 'I'm an area sales manager for Able Cables.'

'You mean you're a salesman?'

'Fuck off!' He laughed. 'I've got a whole team under me,

sunshine. I manage the Stockport branch.' I must have looked blank, because he said, 'Don't tell me you've never heard of Able Cables?'

I smiled apologetically and shook my head.

He tutted. 'We're only the biggest supplier of ACD industrial in the North West.'

'Really?' I said.

He nodded proudly. 'Sonic, Plutonic or Euro-Dynamic: you name it, we sell it.'

I smiled, pretending to be impressed. He regarded me seriously. 'You haven't got a fucking clue what I'm talking about, have you?'

I admitted defeat. He emitted a raucous cackle. 'Still the same old bullshitter, I see. Are you married?'

I told him about Gina, but not Natalie.

'I've been a dad since last Christmas,' he beamed. I raised my plastic cup to him. 'And you'll never guess who I'm married to: Sharon Strong!'

'Who's Sharon Strong?'

He raised his eyebrows. 'What? She's only been made Fitness Instructor of the Year. She was Amateur Step-Aerobics Champion of 1992. She's got her own gym in Hyde. You *must* have heard of "Sharon's Fitness"!'

'Too working class for me, John,' I replied.

'You cheeky cunt,' he said, then laughed appreciatively. 'I suppose she *is* working class. But she's my kind of woman.'

'You mean you love her?'

'I mean she takes it up the arse and she swallows me glue. What more could I ask for?'

I couldn't help laughing and Bomber chortled along with me. I saw the woman sitting nearby stiffen. Her copy of *Country Life* quivered with indignation.

The train arrived in Macclesfield, and the prim woman left the compartment. I didn't see her alight on the platform, though, and wondered if our unsavoury discourse had offended her so much that she'd sought refuge amongst the peasants in second class.

'What kind of things do you write about?' asked Bomber, as if he really couldn't care less.

'New-man stuff,' I answered.

Bomber looked blank. 'Paul Newman? Or Gary Numan?'

'No . . . you know. Men and their feelings.'

Confusion entered his face. 'What feelings?'

'You know . . . The emotions that men repress . . .'

'How do you mean, exactly?' He was frowning as if he thought I was trying to trick him.

I squirmed in my seat. 'Real emotions,' I said. 'Like loving a man, but not being able to show it.'

'*Loving a man?*'

'Come on, John. You must know about feminism?'

'Eh?'

I felt myself blushing slightly. 'Feminism. *Everyone*'s heard of feminism . . .'

'Well, I fucking haven't.'

'Feminism? Sexual politics? The Women's Movement? The belief that women have equal value to men?'

He snorted dismissively. 'I think you're just being silly now, aren't you?'

I gave up. 'Anyway, that's what I do. I write articles about men and women, men and pain, men and sex . . .'

His face lit up. 'Ah. *Now* you're talking.'

'What do you mean?'

'Shagging. I could tell you some stories about the women I've shagged . . .' He left the statement hanging in the air suggestively. A large-bottomed matron waddled past us. In an embarrassingly loud voice Bomber said, 'I wouldn't like to see inside *her* knickers.' He laughed again. I pretended to be amused, while secretly feeling shocked and dismayed. It was like travelling back in time. I realized that Bomber hadn't read a book or absorbed a new idea since he was sixteen years old.

When the train reached Stockport, Bomber and I exchanged telephone numbers. He promised to phone me some time. Perhaps we could go out for a drink? I agreed, convinced that he was just making social noises. At the ticket barrier we parted company. As I headed towards the car-park, he shouted after me, 'Loving a man? You queer bastard!'

Then he laughed and walked away.

In January, everything started to fall apart.

Gina had been miserable and withdrawn all Christmas. I thought she was missing her mother. On Twelfth Night, after we'd taken down the decorations, she began to sob and clutch her stomach. Then her period started. Gina had always suffered from painful periods, but this one was a real, heavy bastard. After she'd been in bed for two days, we called out the family doctor, a fatherly man with nice grey hair and kind eyes behind metal-framed spectacles, who prescribed some Valium and told his patient to call again if she didn't feel better in a week or so.

Outraged, Natalie and I sought a second opinion. Gina had no say in the matter. It only occurs to me now that Natalie and I were treating a grown woman like a child, and that this was a rather peculiar way for two alleged feminists to behave.

We took Gina to a new doctor, a woman, who examined her and came to the surprising conclusion that my wife was possibly pregnant. Gina supplied a urine sample, which was sent off for analysis. The results were negative. It seemed like a false alarm. But Natalie and I were starting to wonder.

One afternoon, while Gina was taking a nap, I had an emergency meeting with Nat in the kitchen. It was pissing down outside. It was one of those winter days when dusk starts to fall before you've got out of bed. We sat at the kitchen table, sipping fennel tea (Natalie didn't want her baby to develop a taste for caffeine). Her once-angular face was growing rounder. Her eyes were huge, dark and full. So was her belly. At five months, it was starting to look as if she was carrying an entire football team around inside her.

'What do you think?' I said.

'I think it's a bit worrying,' said Natalie in a calm, measured voice. 'Last August, she was really pleased for me. And pleased for herself. Remember? In fact, she actually said, "Won't it be great to have some happiness in this house again?"'

'I know,' I said. 'I was there.'

Natalie went on, 'At the same time, she swore blind that she wasn't ready for motherhood herself. But as soon as I start to show, what happens? She gets pains in her womb. A doctor examines her and thinks she might be pregnant. Except there's no baby. Bit strange, don't you think?'

'You mean it might be a sympathetic pregnancy?'

She sighed expressively. 'More of an *unsympathetic* pregnancy. Guy, I've got a funny feeling about all this. Maybe I've just been horribly, horribly selfish. What if Gina wanted a baby more than she ever realized? And now has to sit back and watch me having the child that she feels should have been hers?'

'You think she might be jealous?'

'Yeah. I fucking would be. Just look at the way things have gone for her. She was always a better musician than me. That's not modesty: it's a cold, hard fact. I'm good, but she was brilliant. She screws up her chances because she can't fucking relax. About anything. And what happens? I go to the Royal College, she stays at home. Then I have the first baby, and the father is the man she's married to. Shit!'

She slapped her hand against her forehead in self-reproach. 'I'm an idiot!'

'She hasn't said anything to me about it.'

'What? About me being an idiot?'

'No. About the baby . . . about it being a mistake and everything . . .'

'She doesn't need to. Any fool can tell she's suffering. You'll have to talk to her, Guy. Find out if I'm right.'

After some consideration, I said, 'I think we should *both* talk to her.'

She nodded coolly. 'OK. Let's do it today.'

That night, Natalie and I sat Gina in front of the living-room fire and asked her what was wrong. At first she was spiky and defensive.

'You know what's wrong. I get bad period pains. It happens to millions of women.'

Natalie said, 'But what about when you're not having a period? You're not happy then, either, are you? It's impossible to talk to you at the moment. All we get are one-word answers.'

'Rubbish,' snapped Gina.

'Gina, love,' I said. 'Natalie's right. You've been as miserable as fuck since December. Come on. What's the matter?'

There was a long silence. She lowered her eyes and began to weep silently. Natalie and I drew closer and created a wall of love around her, just as the members of my men's group did around Malcolm every month. But unlike Malcolm, Gina wasn't repulsive, didn't smell and had genuine cause for sorrow.

After a number of false starts, she succeeded in telling us what was weighing her down. 'You're right,' she said. 'You're both right. At first, I thought it'd be fine, but it isn't. I thought I wouldn't mind if it was my own sister. But seeing Natalie getting bigger and bigger, and knowing it's your baby, Guy. I can't stand it.'

Softly, Natalie said, 'You mean it hurts.'

'No,' said Gina. 'I mean I *can't stand it*.'

The Fifth Secret

Gina and I went to bed early. But we were too sad to fuck. So we lay awake in the dark. I asked Gina what she wanted to do. She thought we should go away for a while.

I brightened. 'That's a great idea,' I said. 'We could just take off. Two weeks' holiday would do you the world of good.'

'No,' she answered. 'I don't mean a holiday. I want to move away. Live somewhere else for a while. Till I've sorted myself out.'

'But that's crazy,' I said. 'This is your home. The mortgage is paid and everything.'

Huffily she said, 'Why ask me what I want to do if you're not prepared to listen?'

'I *am* prepared to listen. I just don't think that running away is a very good way of dealing with problems.'

'All right. I'll go on my own, then.'

'Don't get cross. All I'm saying is that I think we ought to stay and tough this one out. I really do. You haven't got any family. Natalie's all you've got. She needs you as much as you need her. At the moment she probably needs you more. She's your sister, Gina. She isn't going to go away. Nor is the baby.'

'I know. So I'll go away instead.'

'No, love. We can't leave Natalie on her own.'

Gina sighed. Her profile was lit by the glow from the street-lamp outside our window. She was lying on her back, staring at the ceiling. 'Guy, haven't you worked it out yet?

Natalie can look after herself. She can cope better than either of us. She *always could.*'

I didn't want to move. It struck me as fucking ridiculous to pay rent to live somewhere I didn't want to live, when we were living rent-free in a house I loved. But I was mature enough to recognize that what I did or didn't want had nothing to do with it. Not really. All that mattered was preventing Gina from feeling any more unhappy than she already felt. This isn't as selfless as it sounds. Her depression was beginning to depress me. I didn't want to feel any worse.

We talked it over with Natalie, who said that she didn't want Gina or me to go, but that Gina should be true to her own feelings. Natalie said that she valued solitude, and had friends, some big fat dykes, that she could invite round if she ever felt lonely. Except she didn't use the expression 'big fat dykes'. That was just me being small-minded.

Gina had always fancied the idea of living in London. With a show of energy and resolve that took her sister and me by surprise, she rang an old schoolfriend who had married and moved to Tottenham and arranged to stay with her for a few days while she looked for somewhere to live. I explained that I was too busy to accompany her, hoping to put her off the idea. But Gina just shrugged and said she'd go alone.

Natalie and I waved her off on the train, still treating her like a child, even when she was in the process of shaping her own destiny. Then, perplexed, we went home to consult Rose's tarot cards. We brewed some tea and sat cross-legged on the floor in the living room, while Natalie separated the trumps from the lesser arcana. Then she laid the cards before me, face down, and asked me to cut them. I did so, she repeated the operation four times, until there were five cards on the floor in the shape of a Calvary cross.

'OK,' said Natalie. 'The card in the centre represents you. The way you are at this time of your life.'

'I'm not interested in me,' I said. 'I thought we were asking about Gina.'

'How can we? She isn't here. But I think we can safely assume that your destiny and Gina's destiny are one.' She gave me a long, slow appraisal. 'Wouldn't you agree?'

I nodded. She turned over the central card. It showed a naked male figure hanging upside down. It was the Hanged Man. 'Ah. I wonder,' said Natalie. 'Does that seem like you?'

I peered down at the card. 'I hope not. He hasn't got a dick.'

'It's not a card about being dickless. It represents self-induced suffering,' said Natalie. 'Self-sacrifice. See? The Hanged Man has probably hung himself. It could be about you leaving here just to please Gina.'

She placed her hand on the card below. 'This is what lies beneath you, what you've truly made your own.'

She turned the card over. It was the Fool. Natalie raised her eyebrows slightly.

'Great,' I said. 'I've made stupidity my own. I'm truly stupid.'

'It could be talking about holy folly,' she said. 'The kind of divine innocence that saints sometimes have. But I can't see that it means that in your case.'

'Thanks, Nat. Thanks a fucking bunch.'

Deftly, she flicked over the card nearest to me. It was Fortune, and showed a spinning wheel with Egyptian deities riding on it. 'This is above you . . . the force that governs your entire fate.'

Smiling at her, I said, 'That's good, isn't it? Doesn't that mean good luck?'

She didn't smile back. 'Well . . . that's up to you. What fortune really means is a *change* of fortune. So if you don't feel lucky, yes, the card probably means good fortune. But if you think you're already lucky, then it means you'll soon be in deep shit.'

'No,' I said emphatically. 'I don't think I'm "already lucky". Not with this situation between you and Gina. Am I fuck lucky!'

She sipped her tea, staring at me darkly over the cup. 'It's all so subjective,' she pointed out. 'What *is* luck, anyway? A Somalian who was watching his entire family starve to death might say you were the luckiest man alive. He wouldn't draw any distinction between you and a person with millions.'

'That's obvious,' I said irritably.

She revealed the card to her right. It was the Empress, Gina's card, my favourite card in the pack. She was the Great Mother, and represented love, compassion, sweetness and fulfilment and joy. 'Hey,' I enthused. 'The Empress is in front of me!'

'No,' said Natalie. She shook her head gravely. 'She's behind you, Guy. The card to my right shows the influence that is about to depart.'

'Bollocks!' I complained. 'Do you believe that? I don't believe that.'

She turned over the final card. 'This is your future,' she announced. The way things were going, I fully expected it to be Death or the Tower or Instant Castration, even though there was no such card as Instant Castration. But the last card turned out to be the Priestess, the initiator, the woman who holds the key to the higher mysteries of the universe. It was the card that had always reminded me of Natalie.

I prayed that Gina would fail to find a flat in London, return home dejected and never refer to the matter again. But on her second night away, she phoned in a jubilant mood to inform me that she'd put down a deposit and a month's rent

71

on a one-bedroom flat in a place I'd never heard of called Crouch End.

It was cold that night: a heavy frost settled on the roads and lawns of the neighbourhood. We knew that Gina wouldn't be home until noon of the following day, so Natalie and I went for a long walk.

There was a junior school at the end of Shepley Drive, the school that Gina and Natalie had both attended as children. Nat and I strolled around the pale frozen playing field, drawn together by the certainty that we would soon be pulled apart. We held hands, or rather linked gloves, while the stars paraded over us like actors in a heartless Hollywood pageant.

'Fuck,' said Natalie. 'This shouldn't be happening. This isn't what I wanted at all.'

'Me neither,' I said.

We peered through a window of the schoolhouse into a dark, empty classroom. The walls of the classroom were lined with paintings by its pupils, jolly daubs that might have been painted by children from any time. We could dimly discern a hand-written sign above the exhibited works that read: MY FAMILY. The painting nearest the window showed a little smiling orange monkey between two big smiling monkeys.

'See that? When our child's old enough to paint a picture like that, I want you and Gina to be in it,' announced Natalie solemnly. 'I don't want it to be just me in the picture. Not just some stick woman in a skirt holding a little kid's hand.'

Later that night, as I was dozing off to sleep, I heard the creak of a floorboard. Startled, I jerked my head up from the pillow, saw a pale shape lowering itself into my bed. It was Natalie. She was wearing a long white night-dress.

'What's the matter?' I whispered.

In a drowsy voice she said, 'Cold.'

She lay on her side, shivering, her arms around me, her big belly pressed against my back. I immediately got a massive hard-on. I could feel it straining to escape from my pyjamas. But what could I do? What did she want me to do? I knew I couldn't touch her without some clear sign of encouragement, so I lay still and waited.

Then she did a strange thing. I was lying on my left side. She eased her right hand into my pyjama jacket and held it over my breast. Her hand was freezing cold. She pressed it against me and I felt my heart pulsing nervously against her palm. 'I can feel your heart,' she mumbled.

'Take it,' I said. 'It's yours.' I immediately felt ashamed, because I'd unintentionally paraphrased the lyric of an embarrassing popular song. But Natalie's only response was a soft, contented moan. Then she fell asleep, her hand growing warm against my chest.

I didn't move, in case she took her hand away. Nor did I dare to wank as she slept, although I was bursting to come, because she was too clever and would know what I was doing. Even if the subtle movement of my elbow failed to wake her, I felt sure that she would know. So I lay paralysed, a hostage to my own cunning.

I felt her breath coming softly against the back of my neck, and the weight of her thighs under mine, and all night long, my buttocks were roasted by the raw heat pouring from her crotch.

I was in Paradise.

I closed my eyes, determined not to waste these precious hours on sleep, but when I opened them again it was nine in the morning and I could hear Natalie clattering about in the kitchen.

Gina and I moved to London a week later. I put it off as long as I could, making excuses about not feeling ready to leave my men's group. 'We need each other,' I said. 'I'd go mad if I didn't have those guys to talk to once a month.'

Gina listened to this drivel calmly, then suggested that if it meant that much to me, why leave the group at all? I could return once a month to attend my meetings. I had no answer to this. So we loaded up all the possessions we couldn't do without, and left the rest behind. Natalie made sure she was out when we departed. She didn't want a tearful scene. We'd shed all our tears the night before.

The journey took six hours. When we arrived at the flat, I couldn't believe my eyes. My new home consisted of two rooms and a miniscule bathroom on the first floor of a crumbling Victorian house. 'Gina,' I said. 'What are you playing at? You've brought me to a fucking slum!'

'The rent's quite low for the area,' she countered.

'I don't care,' I said. 'We don't need to be paying rent at all. We've got a nice house in Hazel Grove.'

We were carrying boxes up a reeking communal staircase. A young couple overtook us and nodded shyly as they admitted themselves to a tiny room next to ours. We nodded, smiled, and continued our argument as soon as their door had closed behind them.

'I knew you were going to do this!' fumed Gina. 'I just *knew* it.'

'Knew I was going to do what?'

'Turn on me! You wait until we get to London, and then you turn on me.'

We unpacked our battered possessions, arguing all the while. I finally apologized to Gina, admitted that she was right, that it wasn't fair for me to say we could move if she found a flat, and then to blame her because the flat was a festering shithole. Privately, I feared that she was losing her sanity.

*

74

The next day, the third Sunday after Epiphany, we decided to see the sights. That afternoon, we caught the W7 bus from Crouch Hill into Finsbury Park, then travelled to Oxford Circus on the Victoria Line. From there, we walked hand in hand down Regent Street to Piccadilly Circus, then on to Trafalgar Square. Then down to the river at Embankment, the filthy grey Thames rolling past us on its way to St Paul's. We arrived at Westminster in time to hear Big Ben strike five, then walked up the Mall to Fuckingham Palace. The Queen wasn't home, or we might have called round to discuss socialism with her.

Then on to Victoria, where there were people lying on the pavement. As we passed, a group of them asked us for change in calculatedly infirm voices, then shouted, 'Fuck off!' when we walked by without stopping. But Gina had been saving our small change to spend on candles in Westminster Cathedral. 'I'll light a candle for Natalie. And a candle for us,' she said. 'And one for the homeless.'

'But not the homeless who shout, "Fuck off",' I advised. 'They can light their own fucking candles.'

Crouch End itself is not so much a place as a series of traffic jams where four busy roads converge: a square mile of rotting Victorian houses, traffic fumes and SAVE OUR LIBRARY stickers, its humming streets thronged by awful women in woolly hats and purple wellies wheeling pushchairs that contain depressed children, also wearing woolly hats and purple wellies. The shops and avenues of this alleged 'village' appear regularly in BBC drama serials, not because all BBC serials are set in Crouch End, but because the directors and producers of these programmes live in Crouch End, and foolishly assume that anywhere they inhabit must be interesting enough to film.

The producers and directors live in complete refurbished

houses, with only one doorbell per entrance. All the aspiring artists, actors, musicians and poor impoverished bastards live in the houses next door – buildings that have been converted into as many flats as possible. At night these dwellings pound and vibrate to the sound of warring TVs and stereos.

Gina and I lived in such a house. An old hippy lived upstairs. He had lived there alone for seventeen years, with his childhood toys, Joan Baez records and home-made musical instruments. Every night at midnight it was his custom to lament the fate of the earth in a tuneless, reedy voice, accompanying himself on an old Spanish guitar. It sounded like a prolonged, agonizing death rattle set to music. If I complained, he stopped, and apologized sweetly. But sometimes it was better to let him sing, because he distracted my attention from the two drunken actors who lived in the flat below.

In the day they 'rested', and at night they ran about beneath us, drunk and rowdy, playing tick and shouting out bizarre things like 'France! Bewilder me, O Shepherd!' More commonly, they shouted, 'Fuck them! Fuck them all!' I tried everything, from stamping on the floor to threatening them with physical violence. On the occasions when I adopted the latter approach, the actors would disarm me by inviting me in for cups of tea or, if their Giros had arrived, cans of warm lager. Calling upon all their dramatic skills, they would then attempt to persuade me that they were not selfish, inconsiderate bastards at all; merely deserving young men who had been driven to drink by a harsh, uncaring world. I would listen, drink up and leave, touched by their joblessness and their apparent sincerity. But the very next night, just as I was dropping off to sleep, I would hear someone cry, 'Fuck them! Fuck them all!' and the nightmare would begin again.

Gina slept through all this. Previously, she had been a

light sleeper, yet the car alarms, barking dogs and howling neighbours of North London served only to lull her into a contented nightly coma.

Gina actually *liked* Crouch End. To me, this was the greatest single proof of her unbalanced mental state. When I complained that we were living in a bourgeois slum, she didn't know what I meant. She kept trying to persuade me to accompany her to a local café on a corner called the Arsehole Café. This wasn't its real name, but O Lord, it should have been, because only arseholes took their custom there. There was a recording studio across the road, called the Arsehole Studio, and famous recording arseholes spent their tea-breaks in the café. These musicians always wore dark glasses and berets to avoid being recognized, then sat right in the window, next to the main road, in the hope of not being recognized by as many people as possible.

Perhaps I'm labouring the point. But I really want you to know how much I hate Crouch End. I would love to throw a grenade into the Arsehole Café and watch all those berets and Ray-Bans flying up into the grey North London sky. I wish I could run around the streets pulling the woolly hats off all the women, unplugging the stereos, shooting the dogs, smearing snot over the only snotless book in the library-that-isn't-worth-saving.

Try to understand. I utterly detest Crouch End, partly for its own sake, but mainly because of what happened next.

Gina tried to get herself together. She really did. First of all, she went to a new-age allergy doctor who put her on a salad and pulse diet that radically improved her health. She also found out about an old converted Church in Camden called St Saviour's, where a charity called the Blackwell Trust helped artists who had lost their way to find it again, not by issuing them with street maps, but by offering them sympathy and encouragement.

It was the kind of charity I'd support if I supported charities. There was a grand piano there, and Gina started visiting the church three days a week to practise performing in front of other people. After her first day she came home glowing with pride because someone had told her how talented she was. I'd been telling her the same thing for years, but she never took me seriously. She thought I was biased.

Natalie rang one afternoon while I was failing, yet again, to write the first page of my *Sexy Secret* serial for *Woman of Today*.

It was lovely to hear Natalie's voice. I'd been missing her, painfully. I told her I believed that soon, next week or next month, we would all be living together again. With hope in her voice, Nat said, 'Why? Has Gina said something?'

'Well, er, not exactly,' I confessed.

I told Natalie about Gina's revived interest in music and the way she'd been playing piano at St Saviour's. I also explained the worthy aims of the Blackwell Trust.

'Wow,' she said. 'That's lovely. That's fantastic.'

But I could tell that she didn't mean this, and that her real thoughts on the subject were akin to mine; namely, that the happier Gina felt in London, the less chance there would be of us all living together under one roof again.

She said abruptly, 'Anyway, I'm not phoning about Gina. I'm phoning to say that someone's been leaving weird messages on the answer-machine.'

'What? Obscene, you mean?'

'No. Just weird. This guy keeps ringing and asking to speak to someone called "Curly".'

The penny took a while to drop. Then I said, 'Hold on a sec. Are you sure that's "Curly"?' Are you sure he isn't saying "Girly"?'

There was a Natalie-length silence. 'What difference does it make? He's talking utter crap, whatever he's saying.'

78

I persisted. Did the caller's name happen to be 'Bomber'? She verified this. I then explained that 'Girly' had been my nickname at Maple Hall Grammar School for Boys. She sighed, as if this only confirmed her prejudices about élitist education.

'Anyway, he wants you to ring him. He's in London all this week, staying at the Yarborough. Do you want the phone number or not?'

I took the number. After a moment's hesitation, I dialled. Bomber sounded overjoyed to hear me. 'Hiya, mate! Hiya! I thought you were fucking me off, pal. I've been phoning you up for a fortnight and only getting a twatting machine. I thought you were just thinking, "I'm a big writer. He's thick. Why should I waste my time on a fat stupid salesman?"'

'No, John,' I lied. 'I'd never think such a thing.'

The Yarborough was not a Yorkshire holiday resort for people with speech impediments, but a luxury hotel in Bayswater. Bomber had a suite on the top floor, overlooking Kensington Gardens. Not that the Round Pond, Peter Pan or the Serpentine Gallery would have meant a thing to him. He wasn't interested in our national heritage, and you only had to look at the size of his arse to see that he hadn't walked anywhere in years.

When I arrived he was sitting on a sofa, watching television in his shirt and underpants. A strikingly pretty young woman with wide cheek-bones and long blonde hair was sitting beside him, writing something in a glossy magazine. She looked Scandinavian. With conspicuous pride, Bomber introduced her as Jo.

'Jo?' I queried.

'Josephine,' grinned Bomber. 'Jo, meet Guy. He was my best friend at school. His shit stinks, and he's very unsightly but he's basically kind-hearted.'

79

Bomber cackled delightedly. Jo extended her hand towards me in a lady-like manner. I took it and bowed. She turned to Bomber and said, 'John, get some trousers on, yer balls is hanging out.'

I realized that she was not Scandinavian at all. She had a high voice and a coarse East End accent.

He looked down at himself. 'You lying cow!'

'They bloody are,' she insisted. 'I can see your testi-whatnots.'

Bomber rang room service to order us some toast and coffee. I sat on a wicker chair by the window while he explained what he was doing in London. 'It's the International Wire and Plug Festival at Earls Court. It's on all this week. I'm supposed to be manning the Able Cables stand. But I'm fucked if I'm going to stand there and talk about cunting cables when I could be shagging Jo up the backside.'

I was shocked by his callousness, and gave Josephine a sympathetic glance to show that I disapproved of my friend's overt sexism. She nodded and grimaced.

Drawing Bomber's attention to the magazine that lay open in her lap, Jo said, 'What shall I put for this one?'

Light-heartedly, Bomber slapped the magazine away. 'I don't fucking know, do I? Ask him. He's supposed to be the brainy cunt.'

She looked uncertain, as if no friend of Bomber's was likely to possess even rudimentary intelligence. 'Is he?' She turned to me. 'Are you brainy like he says?'

'"Are yer briny? Are yer, guv'nor?"' repeated Bomber, mimicking her accent with ruthless accuracy.

'I'm not as thick as him, that's for sure,' I said, making Bomber inhale sharply as if he'd burned his fingers.

She came over to me and showed me the magazine. It was open at a double-page spread, featuring one of those questionnaires that only seem to appear in magazines aimed at teenage girls. And sure enough, the magazine was called *Boy!* Josephine was not a teenager, though. She was about twenty, and, strictly speaking, should have been reading a more intellectual publication like *Woman of Today*.

The subject of the questionnaire was 'Can You Trust Your Boyfriend?' There were about ten questions, each of which had three alternative answers. Readers were invited to mark the likeliest option and tot up their final scores to assess how *loyal their men really were*. If all the answers were 'A's, the magazine claimed, 'Your man is too good to be true. Hang on to him!' Whereas those who scored mostly 'C's were advised, 'I'm afraid your boyfriend has a wandering eye. Ditch him quickly or you're asking for trouble!'

'I'm stuck on number seven,' said Josephine. I took the magazine out of her hands and examined the tricky poser in question. It read:

You are in a club with your boyfriend. While he's at the bar, his ex-girlfriend tries to chat him up. Does he:
a) *Introduce her to you?*
b) *Flirt with her a little, and leave it at that?*
c) *Arrange to meet her secretly when you're safely out of the way?*

I studied the above, struggling to keep contempt out of my face. When I'd finished, I said, 'What's your problem?'

Josephine frowned. 'Well, me problem, you know, is kind of, well, what would John do? He's my boyfriend. But I don't know him well enough to sort of say what he'd do sort-of-fing.'

I meditated for a moment, before saying, 'Let's face it, Jo. He'd do all three. He'd introduce her to you, flirt with her in front of you, and when you'd gone to the toilet, he'd arrange to meet her for sex.'

Bomber didn't hear this. He was in the bedroom, getting

81

dressed. Josephine wriggled impatiently: 'Yeah, I know. So which one should I tick?'

Later, we went out for tea at the Ritz. As soon as the head waiter saw us, you could see him thinking, 'Er, no way.' He strode over and asked if we'd booked in advance, and misery and disappointment darkened his face when Bomber said that we had, and that the name was Lancaster.

It wasn't that we were unwashed or badly dressed, but that we looked as if we deserved to be.

When we were seated, we ordered tea and chose some cholesterol-rich cakes from an ornamental trolley. Then Josephine amazed me by dipping into her bag and removing a shiny new porn mag, which she then passed to me. It was called *Rake*. On its cover there was a picture of a black woman. She was wearing no knickers, bending over and staring between her legs at the reader with an expression on her face that I can only describe as impertinent. I had a strong gut feeling that the photographer had not been Cecil Beaton.

'Have you seen me, yet?' Jo asked with a smile. 'I'm on page eighteen.'

Bomber smirked and nodded.

I said, 'What do you mean?'

She said, 'I'm a model. Ain't he told you? I'm on page eighteen.'

Flabbergasted, I turned to the appropriate page and saw the heading 'Marcella'. Beneath this name was a photograph of a young brunette standing up in a bath tub. She was heavily made-up, with large, pendulous breasts. 'That's not you,' I said uncertainly, 'is it?'

'Yeah, it's me. Yeah, it is. Honest,' Jo assured me shyly.

I turned the page, and saw the same woman on her knees, holding her crotch open for the camera. The caption said: 'This rear view of Marcella should arouse those manly instincts.' The facing page showed 'Marcella' feigning ecstasy as she inserted the handle of a hair-brush into her winkle. Under the photo was a supposed quotation from the model herself.

Hefty handful Marcella says, 'The thing about having big tits is that there's so much you can do with them.' She runs her tongue thoughtfully round her nipples before continuing: 'Mine are really sensitive, and I can often get off just by having them sucked. But I particularly like to wrap them round a big cock and feel that hard rod pulsing away between them. It gives a girl a real feeling of power, knowing that if you keep massaging that stiff prick back and forth it won't be long before a hot, sticky stream of spunk comes shooting out of the end . . .'

I sighed. 'You didn't *really* say that, did you?'
She shook her head grimly. 'No. They went and made all that up. I was dead annoyed when I read it, 'cause I fink it makes me sound a bit tarty . . .'
Bomber sniggered, and Josephine slapped his arm. I said nothing, and turned the page. For the next picture, the photographer had taken such pains to peer up Marcella's birth canal that her face was completely out of focus. The caption read: 'Marcella is no push-over for pretty boys. She says: "I like my men to be old and fat, and even a bit on the ugly side. In fact, the uglier the better."'
I turned to Bomber. 'Now I know what she sees in you.'
'You bastard!' he spluttered, spraying cream cake all over the table-cloth.
I flicked through the pictures again, shaking my head. 'But it doesn't look anything like you, Jo,' I insisted. 'It could be anyone.'
She shrugged. 'I know. They made me wear a wig.'
A waiter arrived with the tea. As he leaned over me he

said in a low voice, 'Please, sir. Put the magazine away. The ladies don't like it.'

I glanced around. The tea-room was full, but no one was paying us the slightest bit of attention. 'What ladies?' I demanded. 'Where?'

'Please, sir. Put it away. Think of the ladies.'

Bomber laughed. 'We *are* thinking of the ladies. We're thinking about their tits and fannies.'

Josephine told Bomber to be quiet and returned the magazine to her bag.

We moved on to an Italian restaurant in Soho, where Bomber introduced himself to the staff as a friend of Luigi. The staff clearly had no idea who Luigi was, but were too polite to say so. Luigi certainly wasn't the manager, and the restaurant itself was called Emilio. Maybe Bomber had taken us to the wrong restaurant by mistake. Whatever the truth, we had a delicious meal.

When we were sipping coffee, I asked Bomber and Josephine how they'd met. Josephine admitted, a little sheepishly, that she had only known Bomber for three days. She'd been hired as the bikini-clad model on the Able Cables stand at the International Wire and Plug Festival at Earls Court. It was her job to wear a bikini and hand out promotional leaflets to passers-by.

'We work as a team,' explained Bomber. 'She sticks her tits out and I hold me stomach in.'

'I don't see what a woman in a bikini has got to do with wires and plugs,' I sneered.

'That just shows how little you know about business, pal,' said Bomber. 'Never underestimate the selling power of the sticky-out nipple.'

'But you haven't been anywhere near Earls Court all day. What if someone finds out?'

Bomber shook his head sagely. 'No one'll miss us. Good cable sells itself.'

I asked Jo why she was handing out leaflets at Earls Court when she had a job as a 'model'. 'I'm only just starting up, kind of fing. You don't get paid much at first. Not on magazines.'

'Why do it at all?'

She leaned her face against her fist while she thought of an answer. After about twenty seconds she said, 'Well, it's kind of difficult to explain, but it was sort of always me ambition because I felt that it was something I needed to do. And I did it for me, not anyone else, 'cause I just wanted to see if I could achieve me ambition. If yer see what I mean.'

I noticed that Bomber was observing her with something akin to pity in his eyes. He patted her hand and added, 'She wants to get into porn films, don't you, love?' He smiled. 'We both do.'

I laughed scornfully. 'Forget it, John. They'd never have you in a porn film.'

He looked offended. 'They fucking would! They'd *have* to have me if me and Jo were a partnership. We'd be like a husband-and-wife shagging team.'

'Except you've already got a wife.'

'Yes, big-mouth,' retorted Bomber. 'Jo knows I'm married, so you can go and fuck yourself.'

But the Chianti had gone to my head. I couldn't let it go. He was making me angry. I said, 'Yeah. Some gimmick, John. A husband-and-wife shagging team, with a wife who looks like an angel and a husband who looks like a pot-bellied pig.'

To my amazement, both Bomber and Josephine burst into merry laughter. They laughed until their faces were streaming. At last, wiping his eyes, Bomber squeezed Jo's shoulder and said, 'I love this lad. Don't you? Don't you just fucking love him?'

We caught a taxi, and Bomber made the driver cruise around until he found an off-licence that sold real Bourbon. Since his childhood, Bomber had always admired America and the American way, and now he was destroying his liver in the American way by assaulting it with large tumblers of neat Kentucky whiskey.

It was about nine in the evening, on a wet, black winter's night. I told Bomber and Jo that I'd had a great time, but really ought to be getting home to Gina. But they begged me, literally *begged* me to return to the Yarborough with them for a few drinks. When we reached Bomber's suite, Bomber and Jo started on the Bourbon. I had a brandy from the mini-bar. Bomber and Jo huddled together on the sofa, whispering like school-children and giggling.

'I know you're talking about me,' I slurred. 'Don't pretend you aren't.'

Jo and Bomber seemed to reach some kind of decision. They kissed each other. Then Jo bounced to her feet and skipped into the bathroom. Bomber leant forward in the way that drunks have when they're confiding in you. 'I tell you, pal, you've got it cracked, there.'

'Eh? Whadya mean?'

'What do you think I mean? She fucking fancies you. She thinks you've got a bit of decorum.'

'Why? Because I can spell "antelope"?'

'Fuck off and listen. Ever had a threesome, Guy?'

My heart-rate accelerated. 'What? Are you serious?'

'Yeah. Three-in-a-bed. How about it? I've got some poppers.'

'Poppers?'

'You know . . . those pills that gays take to get their rocks

86

off. They relax you . . . make you feel everything. And it's not as if you don't want to shag her. I know you do, 'cause I've seen you looking at her tits, you unsubtle slob.'

I felt myself blushing, yet I was not embarrassed. I was excited. And extremely scared.

'Come on, Guy,' said Bomber. 'I'd like you to fuck my girlfriend. And she'd love you to fuck her. And you know as well as I do that you'll never forgive yourself if you don't fuck her.'

'No, John. Thanks, but no.'

'I've got enough rubbers, if that's what's worrying you. Strawberry flavour, licorice, and even the old-fashioned kind that taste like incontinence pants.'

'No. I can't do it.'

Bomber introduced a fatherly tone into his voice. ''Course you can. 'Course you can, mate. She's having a shower. She'll be out in a minute. Don't commit yourself, yet. Take your time. See how you feel. If you don't want to do anything, you don't have to . . .'

My friend, forgive me if I suspend my narrative at this juncture to offer you the kind of questionnaire of which Josephine herself is so tragically fond. The title of this questionnaire is 'Can You Trust Guy Lockheart?' If your answer to my questions is invariably 'A', then 'Hang on to me, because I'm too good to be true'. If your score consists mainly of Cs, you are advised to ditch me forthwith, because I have a wandering eye.

1) Josephine enters the room naked and dripping wet. Then she proceeds to dance provocatively, before masturbating with an empty wine bottle. Do I:
a) *Avert my eyes and sing a Cliff Richard song?*
b) *Make my excuses and leave?*
c) *Get a massive erection?*

2) Josephine takes me by the hand and leads me into the bedroom. Bomber follows. He throws off his clothes and lies on the bed with Josephine. Do I:

a) *Phone my wife and tell her what is happening?*

b) *Watch from a safe distance?*

c) *Hurriedly undress and join them on the bed?*

3) Encouraged by Bomber, Josephine attempts to make love to me. Do I:

a) *Tell her that I wouldn't have got undressed at all had I known what she had in mind?*

b) *Phone Cliff Richard and tell him what is happening?*

c) *Have athletic, exciting sex with Jo. Then see a vision of Gina's face as I reach orgasm, realize what I've done and immediately feel sadder than hell?*

The Sixth Secret

Gina knew.

Not because she saw me in a dream, grinning like an ape as the ferryman rowed me through Traitor's Gate. Not because she smelled cheap perfume on my clothes, or heard a thin disembodied voice whisper the name 'Josephine' in her ear.

She simply *knew*.

I staggered home some time after four in the morning, expecting to find her waiting up for me. But she was in bed, softly snoring. I undressed in the dark and climbed into bed beside her, smelling Josephine's sharp, sweet smell under my finger-nails. That smell pursued me into a dreadful, chaotic half-sleep, so that when I awoke at nine, I felt as if I'd spent the night running up and down a flight of stairs in a tall derelict building.

Gina was waiting for me in the other room. As I slouched through, white-faced and crumpled, the kettle was boiling. She laid a plate of toast at my place on the table. The toast was thickly spread with cherry jam, my favourite. 'Eat it while it's hot,' she said.

Then she sidled over to the kettle, brought it back to the boil, and poured steaming water into a large tea-pot. She tipped some milk into a mug, then placed the mug and the pot before me.

'How was Bomber?' she asked. It sounded like a polite enquiry: nothing more.

'Oh, drinking too much. Thinking too little.' I forced a smile. 'You know Bomber.'

'No, I don't,' she replied. 'What are you talking about? I've never met him.'

'Oh,' I said, unsteadied by the sharpness of her response. 'Oh. Yeah. So you haven't.'

I switched on the radio and tried to act normal. In the morning 'normal' for me means listening to the radio, eating breakfast and not talking. But I definitely didn't feel normal, because I was aware of her eyes upon me. When I'd finished my toast and was on my second mug of tea, she suddenly said, 'OK. Who was she?'

I glanced up at her sharply. She looked perfectly calm and ordinary; no more pale or dishevelled than anyone else who has just got out of bed. But I didn't like the way she was staring.

'Who was who?' I said.

'The woman you were with last night. What's her name?'

I tried to say that I'd been with Bomber, not a woman, but I was so alarmed that I gulped nervously in the middle of the sentence. She noted my reaction, and I saw pain flicker across her face.

Then I heard myself tell Gina the truth. To this day, I don't know what possessed me. Perhaps I imagined that there was nothing to be afraid of. When I spoke, my own voice sounded strange and muffled, as if I was somehow removed from myself, eavesdropping on someone else's tragic conversation.

'Her name's Josephine,' I said. 'She's Bomber's girlfriend.'

She nodded, as if this was hardly news. 'What did you do with her?'

'I didn't want to . . . we got drunk. I hardly knew what I was doing. I'm really sorry. Really.'

Her hand shot across the table towards me and I flinched, expecting a blow. But all she did was remove a scrap of toast from my chin with her finger and drop it on to my plate.

90

'Do you mean you can't remember what you did with her, or just won't tell me?'

I sighed. I was beginning to perspire. 'Fucking hell, Gina, I'm not going to answer that. What do you want to know for? It won't happen again. Don't. Stop torturing yourself.'

After a pause, she said, 'What was she like?'

'I've told you, I'm not go—'

'I don't mean in bed,' she snapped, showing the first sign of disquiet. 'I mean as a person.'

I was tempted to paint a wholly unattractive portrait, but recalling the sweet, silly face above that pornographic body, I could not bring myself to bear false witness. 'She's pretty. Working class. Not educated. But not malicious in any way. Completely without malice. You'd probably like her.'

Gina looked at me for a while, frankly. 'I'm glad you haven't lied to me. I would have hated you to lie.'

We sat in silence while I waited for her next question. Having said so much, we were both compelled to carry on. It was like *Mastermind*, that TV quiz programme, where Magnus says, 'I've started, so I'll finish.' That was Gina and I. We'd started, so we had to finish.

Gina said, 'What does she look like?'

'Gina, don't . . .'

'No. I want to know. What does she look like?'

'Oh, fuck.' I sighed again, but knew it was a perfectly reasonable question. 'She's blonde. Long blonde hair. Just what you'd expect from Bomber.' Then I remembered that she hadn't met him, so I added, 'If you knew him, that is. She's . . . you know on *Blind Date*, when Cilla asks the guy to describe his ideal woman? Well, that's what she looks like.'

Blind Date was one of Gina's favourite TV programmes. She said, 'Blonde hair, big tits, tiny waist, long legs?'

It sounded so fucking sordid, spelled out like that. Reluctantly, I said, 'Yeah. That's what she's like.'

91

She tutted, as if she'd expected better from me. 'Oh, Guy. Is that what you really want?'

'No. Is it hell! They got drunk, and they forced me to join in.'

'*How* did they force you?'

'All right. They didn't force me. But I was drunk, too.'

'Too drunk to know what you were doing?'

'Yeah.'

She tilted her head at a sceptical angle.

'No,' I admitted.

'You'd better not see either of them again,' she warned.

I was elated. Was it going to be *that* easy? 'I know,' I said with unseemly eagerness. 'I won't.'

'I mean it, Guy.'

'Yeah. So do I. No question.'

'Right.' She got to her feet and cleared away my dishes. 'I'd better get a move on.'

Panic seized me. 'Why? Where are you going?'

She turned and looked at me. The sunlight caught her head, and I saw a few grey hairs in her fringe that I hadn't noticed before. 'Why?' she asked me. 'Do you care?'

'God, Gina, of course I do.'

'It's Friday,' she said. 'I'm going to St Saviour's. I'll be back at tea-time. Then we can talk properly.'

'Wait,' I said. 'How did you know? You haven't told me how you knew.'

She shrugged. 'It's hard to explain.'

'Try. I want to know.'

'When I woke up, you were still asleep,' she said. 'I looked at your face and hardly recognized you. You looked like a completely different person.'

'What kind of person?'

'I've told you. Someone I didn't know. And wouldn't *want* to know.'

'What else?'

'Nothing else. That's it.'

'You just looked at me and knew? I don't believe you.'

'I don't believe *you*, either.' Wearily, she selected a clean towel from a basket by the fridge. With her back to me, she said, 'I have to admire you, though. You did it brilliantly. You fooled just about everybody.'

An unpleasant thought occurred to me. 'Are you going to tell Natalie?'

That was too much for her. She finally lost her cool. She turned on me, virtually spitting poison. 'Why would I want to do that, *Guy*?' She made my name sound like a venereal wart. 'What the hell has it got to do with Natalie?'

She dragged an armful of clothes out of the ironing pile, hurled them ineffectually around the room, and stormed out. It was then that I realized that she knew exactly how I felt about her sister, had known for some time, and that the three of us would not live together again. Not next week, next month, not ever.

I had all day to think about what had happened. I saw that I'd forgotten who Gina really was. Because she was accident-prone and a little neurotic, I'd grown to think of my wife as being mentally unstable, not realizing that she may merely have been reacting sanely to an insane situation. (Anyway, who am I to talk about sanity? How sane is it to live one's entire life pretending to be another person?)

The truth about Gina was that she was possessed of a deep, intuitive intelligence. Yes, she was vulnerable – a lot of intelligent people are. But she was no fool. Yet since Rose's death, Natalie and I had come to think of Gina as a kind of silly mascot: someone to protect and patronize. When, in reality, my little wife had seen through us both, and been so disturbed by what she saw that she ran away to London, like a character in a story book.

Natalie and I were two deeply selfish people. Gina had

been stifled by us. And now she had her own life to lead. I wanted to be part of that life. I still loved her. But I didn't see how we could progress unless we were honest with each other.

Yet the truth would have destroyed her. Without wishing to sound like Vaughan from my men's group, I do believe that some truths are best left unspoken. For instance, how could I tell Gina that I wanted to have sex with her sister every day for the rest of my life? What good would that have done? Nor could I admit that our own sex life had been unsatisfactory from the outset.

That was another thing: Josephine had been the best sexual partner I'd ever had. Everything about her, from the way she moved and sighed, to the softness of her skin and the way she faked her orgasms, had been absolutely perfect. We had nothing to say to each other, but in bed we had reached an immediate understanding.

Gina shared my ideals. Jo didn't know what an ideal was. But she knew how to suck a cock. Gina had never liked sucking cocks, or my cock at least, and she'd always had a demoralizing habit of reaching for the tissues two seconds after I'd ejaculated. Sex had always been far too messy for her. She hated getting the sheets wet. Of course, we always had great conversations after we'd had sex. But not much fun while we were actually doing it.

How can you tell a person such things? It's bad enough just to think them. I imagine that Gina thought that I was crap in bed, too. But I didn't want to discuss it. No one ever does. I'm sure that the world is full of people like Gina and me: couples who really love each other, but hardly ever screw because one or both of them are lousy at sex. Or just plain bored.

You want the truth? I'll give you the truth.

I was in love with Gina, but I didn't want to fuck her. I

94

wanted to fuck Josephine, but I didn't want to talk to her. I was in love with Natalie, and I also wanted to fuck her, but I wasn't sure that I *liked* her.

I stayed in the flat all day, sick to my stomach, dreading Gina's homecoming. At around five, the phone rang. I picked it up, and a squeaky London voice said: 'Could I speak to Guy, er, Lock ... oh I can't read me own writing ...'

'Jo?' I said. 'Is that you?'

'Yeah,' she said. 'It is. It's me.'

'How did you get this number?'

'John gave it me. Dincha want me to ring yer?'

'Well ... it's a bit difficult,' I said. 'I'm married, remember.'

'Oh,' she said, deflated. 'Doncha want to see me then?'

'What do you mean? You're going out with John, aren't you?'

'Yeah. But John's gone home to his wife, ain't he? So I got nuffink to do.'

I sighed. 'It's not a good time, Jo. I can't really talk just now.'

'Oh.' She sounded sad. 'Doncha want me to ring yer, then?'

Weakly, I said, 'Well ... That's up to you.'

There was a long pause. I could hear her breathing noisily into the receiver like a small child. She said: 'Doncha like me, then?'

'Yeah, sure, I like you a lot. It's not about liking you.'

There was a second, longer pause. 'Whatsit about, then?'

'Jo, ring me another time. OK?'

'When?'

'I don't know. Just not now.'

I could hear her listening at the end of the line. I knew that she had no intention of hanging up, so I gently replaced the receiver. Cursing, I made myself a drink. Then the phone rang again. I picked it up, expecting to hear Gina's voice. But it was Josephine.

'Guy?' she said. 'Is that you?'

'Jo, what are you doing?'

Suspiciously, she said, 'Nuffink. Why? What are you doing?'

'Listen, Jo,' I said. 'I thought you said you'd ring me another time.'

'Yeah,' she said, confused. 'This *is* another time.'

I prepared an official speech in readiness for Gina's return. It started with an admission of guilt, moved on to the customary assurances about my behaviour being no reflection on my wife's excellence as a companion or a lover, and ended with the promise that I would never stray from the path of righteousness again. It was cowardly nonsense, but a lot less damaging than the truth. Less damaging to me, I mean.

Gina came home while I was watching *Coronation Street*. I felt guiltier than ever when I saw how shockingly pale she looked, assuming that she'd spent the day agonizing over our relationship. But when she climbed on to the bed and lay there, gripping her belly and groaning, I knew that I was wrong, and that her period was on the way again.

I gave her some analgesics, which had no effect. The pain got so bad that I called out a doctor. He arrived an hour later, a pleasant young Asian who gazed around our flat approvingly.

'You wouldn't believe some of the filth and squalor I have to put up with,' he said. 'Dirty dishes, excrement on the floor . . . quite dreadful.'

'Never mind that,' I said. 'My wife's in agony.'

He felt Gina's brow and admitted that her temperature was high. But he wouldn't accept that there was anything seriously wrong with her. Heading for the door, he said, 'I see this often with sensitive people. What is discomfort to others may be unbearably painful to the sensitive.'

'No. Please,' I said, 'won't you examine her?'

Reluctantly, but with good grace, he went back into the bedroom, lifted up her sweater and prodded her sides and belly. Gina cried out in pain, and then sobbed miserably. The doctor followed me into the other room.

'I'm sorry,' he said. 'You were right and I was wrong. There is a large oval swelling on her right ovary. I will write to the hospital immediately, requesting that she see a specialist.'

'What could it be?'

'Ah. She is how old?'

'Twenty-six.'

'And she has no children?'

Puzzled, I shook my head.

'Women's bodies are designed to reproduce, you see. One of the main reasons that Western women have so many problems with their reproductive organs is that they leave it far too late to have children.'

He was a nice man. I didn't want to insult him. So I merely said, 'You're sure about this, are you?'

'Oh, yes,' he said. 'Quite sure. But I'll see that she's put to the front of the queue. The very front.'

There followed a ridiculous conversation in which the doctor asked me what I did for a living, and was greatly impressed by the news that I was a journalist. 'And your wife is a musician? I must say it is a pleasure, a real pleasure, to make the acquaintance of cultured people.'

However, I doubted that he'd think of me as a cultured person if he'd read my work. He gave me his card, in case I ever wanted to write a magazine article about a particularly cultured Asian doctor, then departed.

*

Gina's pain abated before midnight. She was weak and listless all weekend, which meant, thankfully, that my recent fall from grace was not referred to and that I was given the opportunity to be servile and contrite. On the Wednesday of the following week, she was called to the Whittington Hospital in Archway for an examination. A female consultant admitted us to her office and opened the conversation by accusing Gina of queue-jumping. But when she took the trouble to examine the patient, the silly woman promptly changed her tune. 'Dear me,' she said. 'Did you know you've got a swelling here?'

That evening, Gina of the dark eyebrows and the long body and the tiny mole above her upper lip was admitted as an emergency to the Royal Northern Hospital in Holloway Road. I watched while a tall, posh, tired junior doctor called Jeremy gave her yet another examination. She lifted her shirt, enabling him to press his palm into her right side and he said, 'Goodness. Did you know you'd got a swelling here?'

Then, inexplicably, he gave her a full breast examination, rotating his hands around her breasts until their dark-as-mud nipples became erect. He performed this feat with such innocent curiosity that I half-expected him to say, 'Goodness. Did you know you'd got *two* swellings here?'

When the doc had finished amusing himself, he told Gina that the next day, after lunch, she would be operated on. Doctor Jeremy made it sound like a bit of a lark. 'Nothing to worry about. We'll just open you up and have a look inside. It's just a cyst on the ovary. We'll get rid of it for you, and then put you back together again. Nothing to it. All right?'

He went through a form with us, starting by asking her what she was allergic to. She reeled off a long list of foods. 'No, no,' he said. 'I mean things like penicillin . . .'

She shook her head.

'What about your family history?' He raced through a litany of complaints and disabilities. She kept saying, 'No, no, no.' And he scribbled crosses over all the appropriate boxes.

Gina liked Jeremy. I could tell. He was soft, clean and well-spoken – a bit like Cliff Richard. Except that Cliff would never have felt her tits. Unless God had commanded him to. None the less, Jeremy upset her when he announced that after the operation she'd need to be connected to a saline drip. Her cheeks positively flushed with emotion. Then Jeremy's cheeks flushed, in sympathy with hers.

'Just a little nick in the back of your hand,' he reassured her. 'Nothing to worry about.'

When he'd gone, she grabbed hold of me and said, 'Oh, Guy. Please. Don't let them cut me open.' Then she had a good cry. So did I. I held her tight and told her that I loved her, had always loved her, and that I would never make her unhappy again.

For once, I was telling the truth.

I returned to the flat alone, at about nine-thirty in the evening. I suddenly felt incredibly empty and lonely. Gina had asked me not to tell Natalie, because she didn't want Natalie to visit her in hospital, looking pregnant and beautiful. So I rang my parents, and then I rang Ben. Ben didn't know what to say, so passed me on to Rachel, who promised to send flowers and a card.

When the call was over, I felt bad about not phoning Natalie. I pictured her, living all alone in that big dark house in Shepley Drive. She loved her sister, loved us both. She had a right to know. So I disobeyed my wife and tried to contact Natalie, but only got the fucking answer-machine. I listened for the bleeps and said, 'Hiya, Nat. It's Guy. Would you ring back, gorgeous? It's quite important.'

When I rang off, I realized that I'd slipped up and left the word 'gorgeous' on Natalie's answer-machine, recorded on tape so that she could play it back again and again, and hear what an unenlightened slob I really was. But if she ever challenged me, I knew that I could argue that I'd suffered from a momentary lapse of taste, while the balance of my mind had been disturbed.

I went out for a walk, climbing up to Mount View Road, which overlooked the city and St Paul's. I thought it was funny that the only thing worth seeing in Crouch End was St Paul's, which wasn't even in Crouch End. Tonight, the view was marred by a haze of orange smog that blotted out the horizon. I couldn't see the cathedral, so I stood there, admiring the pollution instead. Then I returned to the flat.

As I climbed the stairs, I could hear our phone ringing. I fumbled with my key in the door, afraid that I wouldn't answer it in time. Then I rushed into the flat and snatched up the receiver.

'Hello?'

A woman's voice said, 'Oh. Who's that?'

I said, 'It's me. Guy. Who's that?'

'It's me. Josephine.'

I went to see Josephine. She lived in Hammersmith, where she shared a two-bedroom flat with another girl. It was after eleven by the time I arrived. Jo was on her own. Her flatmate was away, visiting a friend.

'I'm glad ya could come,' said Jo, throwing her arms around my neck. 'I hate bein' on me own.'

I didn't tell her about Gina, because I didn't want to make myself seem unsympathetic. As Ariadne had pointed out, a man can be as sexist as he likes, as long as he's *nice*. What I was doing certainly wasn't nice. But I'm not going to lie to you. I've made up my mind to tell you the truth, even if it makes you hate me.

We went straight to her room. We didn't need a drink to

break the ice. There was no ice to break. Jo asked if I wanted her to dance for me again. I said that I could take or leave the dancing. We undressed and got into bed. It was a single bed that creaked a lot. The pillowcase featured a faded print of Charles and Diana, in the days when they loved each other, or at least pretended to.

I mouth-fucked her, fist-fucked her, drank her and spanked her. I buggered her, fingered her, came on her tits. I came up her cunt, she came in my face. She pissed on me, rode on me, smeared me with juice. When we'd finished, we were both exhausted, it was five in the morning and the mattress was soaking wet.

God forgive me. It had been the most wonderful night of my life.

In the morning, while Jo slept on, I showered, and made it to the hospital by noon. I was expecting to spend some time with Gina before she went into surgery. But her bed was empty. A staff nurse told me that there had been a cancellation, and that Gina had gone down to theatre two hours earlier than planned.

'Then I'll wait,' I said.

The nurse shook her head. 'No point. She'll be out cold for hours. You'll just be sitting around. You might as well go home for an hour or two.'

I went back to the flat, and took the phone off the hook. The house was quiet. The hippy upstairs was out, and the actors downstairs were resting their throats in preparation for another night of shouting, 'Fuck them! Fuck them all!'

I went to sleep for a couple of hours. It was an enjoyable nap, untroubled by dreams or anxieties. When I awoke it was four, and already getting dark. I splashed my face, brushed my teeth, made myself a sandwich which I consumed on the way to the bus stop.

There were no warning signs. The bus driver didn't leer

darkly as I bought my ticket or say, 'Archway? Sorry, sir. This bus goes one way only.' None of the passengers backed away and crossed themselves at the sight of me. It was a perfectly uneventful, unlovely bus ride.

I bought a bunch of daffodils from a flower stall by the tube station, and some magazines from a newsagent on Holloway Road. Then I ran down the busy sloping street to the hospital. Gina's ward was circular in design, with all the beds arranged around the walls like the numerals on a clock. In the centre of the ward was a glass-fronted partitioned office, where the doctors and nurses gathered to sip coffee, sulk and slump into exhausted heaps.

No one saw me enter. I rounded the ward twice, searching in vain for Gina, until Dr Jeremy and the nurse I'd spoken to earlier saw me and came bounding out of the office.

'Mr Lockheart?' panted Jeremy. He looked agitated, and had dark rings around his eyes. 'Mr Lockheart?'

'I can't find her,' I said.

'We've been trying to phone you,' he said. 'Please would you come with me, please?'

'Why?' I said. 'What's the matter?'

The nurse looked at me, but said nothing. Her lips were tightly pressed together, as if she was afraid of what she might say to me.

'What is it? Where is she?' I said, following Jeremy. He didn't answer me. We entered a small windowless side room. He turned on the light and closed the door.

He asked me to sit down. There was only one chair, so he sat on a pile of cardboard boxes.

'I'm very sorry,' he told me.

'Why?' He looked baffled, so I elaborated, 'What are you sorry for?'

'I'm afraid that something awful has happened,' he said. I noticed that his knees were trembling.

'It can't be as bad as that, surely?' I said.

'Yes,' he replied. 'I'm afraid it is, Mr Lockheart.'

Half-joking, I said, 'Why? She isn't dead, is she?'

His eyes filled with water. 'Yes,' he said. 'I'm very sorry. We don't really know what happened. She died before we even had a chance to operate.'

'Who died? Not Gina?'

He nodded, and wrung his hands. 'Yes,' he said. 'She started having respiratory problems. Then she stopped breathing altogether. I was there, Mr Lockheart. I swear we did everything we could.'

'But why?' I said. Jeremy and I were now trembling in unison. 'I thought it was just a cyst. What happened?'

But I could see by his face that Jeremy didn't know. 'We tried everything,' he repeated.

'Where is she? I want to see her,' I said.

'Of course,' said Jeremy, getting to his feet.

'Not just yet,' I said.

Jeremy apologized and sat down again. A student nurse brought in two mugs of strong sweet tea. At first I felt utterly numb. Then, with a sudden thrill, I saw how gloriously tragic it all was: to become a widower at the age of thirty. Dr Jeremy was watching me closely, through tearful blood-shot eyes. I felt he wanted me to cry too, so I obliged him. But I found that I could only produce the kind of self-pitying sobs that the relatives of disaster victims save for TV news cameras, when they know that they may never get another chance to look so heart-broken again.

The real tears came later.

The Seventh Secret

I really miss my wife.
I know it isn't much of a secret, but I needed to tell you.

The Eighth Secret

Ben and Natalie were waiting for me at the station. I was leaning out of the window as the train drew up to the platform. Natalie saw me instantly, and pointed me out to Ben. When the carriage drew to a standstill, they were standing right outside my door, as if the train's sole purpose in coming here had been to deliver me into their care.

We hugged each other. Natalie was wearing a voluminous dark overcoat that I hadn't seen before. The coat belled out in front of her because of the size of her belly. Ben commented on the fact that the train was six minutes late, and we all slagged off British Rail, as if we had nothing better to talk about. Natalie and Ben were holding hands, which shocked me, because they didn't really like each other. They were both grey-faced, as if they hadn't slept for a week, and I could tell by the expression in their eyes that I looked even worse than they did.

We climbed into Ben's crappy third-hand Mercedes. Ben drove and Natalie and I sat in the back. My bag was on my knees, my hands rested on the bag, and Natalie's hands rested on mine.

'They're sending her tomorrow,' I said.

'We know, mate,' said Ben. He sounded a bit choked. 'I'm taking care of it. It's all sorted.'

I could feel them both wondering how and when to broach the subject of the funeral, so I said, 'Have you sorted anything out with the undertaker?'

Natalie said: 'Tuesday.'

This was Thursday night.

I said, 'And is it going to be a proper burial?'

There was a moment of awkwardness. Natalie tightened her grip on my hands. 'We can try if you like. I mean, if that's what you want. But nobody really gets buried any more, Guy.'

'The ground's full, mate,' said Ben seriously.

I laughed and repeated what he'd said, holding him up to ridicule. He looked hurt. 'Oh, fuck it, you know what I mean,' he sighed.

'Ben's right,' said Natalie. 'There isn't the space to bury people any more.'

'It isn't environmentally what-not,' said Ben.

'Friendly,' I offered.

'Yeah,' he nodded. 'That's the one.'

I gave up. I didn't have the energy to argue.

Tentatively, glancing at me in the mirror, Ben said, 'We were wondering where you'll be wanting to stay, mate? Or if you'd given it any thought.'

I was surprised by the question. It seemed obvious to me that my rightful place was with Natalie. Before I could answer she said, 'You know you've always got a home with me. But we weren't sure whether you could face . . .'

She was unable to finish the sentence.

Before I could reply, Ben said, 'Only, we could always put you up at ours for a while. It'd mean kipping on the settee. But you're always fucking welcome. I mean, welcome. I wish I could stop fucking swearing.'

'Thanks, Ben. But it'd seem stupid for us all to pile into your place when Natalie lives in an empty house.'

They both agreed enthusiastically. This was the answer they wanted to hear. On the way home we stopped off to see my parents, who were looking tired and old. They *were* tired and old, but you know what I mean.

It was all rather restrained. Even in the midst of death,

everyone was so hopelessly British. My dad stood up to embrace me, and I thought I saw tears glinting in his eyes, but he quickly blinked them away, lest he be judged weak for showing how desperately sad he was.

That night I returned to the house on Shepley Drive to sleep in the room that Gina and I used to share. The bed and the sheets and the darkness itself seemed to be heavy with her presence. I lay there weeping, thinking about her all alone in hospital, sad and scared, while I'd been having fun with Jo.

There was an icy mournful wind blowing outside the window and I kept praying that Gina would crawl into my bed to warm her feet on me. But Gina wasn't alive any more, and I was bitterly cold all night.

On Sunday afternoon I walked round to see Ben and Rachel. Rachel was frantically worried about me. She was afraid that I might do something drastic, not realizing that I'd already done it. She fed me home-made scones and talked to me about ordinary, everyday things, all the while watching me with bright, anguished eyes. Ben still looked like a young Burt Reynolds. But young Burt Reynolds when he was heart-broken.

Then, as I was telling them about identifying Gina's body in hospital, I disgraced myself by breaking down in front of the entire family. Rachel took the children into another room so that I could be alone with my brother. Ben paced around, kicking the furniture. 'Fuck!' he fumed. 'Fuck!'

When I'd finished sobbing, and Ben had finished kicking the furniture, I told him about Bomber and Jo. I was scared of telling him, because he'd once told me that if I ever fucked things up for Gina, he'd never forgive me. But my men's group didn't meet for another fortnight, and I had to talk to someone.

He listened in silent bemusement. As a child, Ben had

107

always loathed Bomber; loathed him for his customized push-bike, his Levi suits and the balcony outside his bedroom window.

I ended by saying, 'I killed Gina.'

'No,' he said. He shook his head as if he was trying to clear it of judgemental thoughts. 'Did you fuck.'

'I did,' I stressed. 'I betrayed her, and then on the night before she died, I betrayed her again. I think she knew, Ben. Just like she knew when I let her down the first time. Deep inside, she knew, and that's why she died.'

'Bollocks!' he snapped. 'It was the anaesthetic. She was allergic to anaesthetic. That's what the fucking, er, coroner said.'

'Thanks. But I think it was me, Ben.'

'No.' He put his arm round me. 'You were a dickhead. I can't deny that. But you shouldn't blame yourself.'

'Why not?'

He roared: 'Because it was FUCKING BOMBER'S FAULT!'

It snowed on the day of the funeral. It was April, yet it snowed. Gina had always loved snow, so I hoped that this was a good omen. A good omen? My wife was about to be cremated, and there was I, looking for good omens.

Natalie was eight months pregnant. There were six of us in the funeral car: Natalie and me, Rachel and Ben, Mum and Dad. Rachel's mum was looking after the children. Our car followed the flower-laden coffin to Norbury Church, where its occupant had once been a member of the Young Christian Fellowship. I wondered if she had ever told her young fellow Christians that she believed in Jesus, but not in God.

I wasn't sure that the vicar believed in God, either. He tried to tell us that God had taken Gina to his bosom because she was such a great girl. But he said it as if he was thinking, 'I know this is crap, and you know it's crap, but I can't just stand here and say nothing.'

He went on to say, 'Some people think that there's no heaven, no afterlife, and that when we die that's it. The end. Over and out. To which I say, "Yuk!"' Then he paused meaningfully, as if waiting for the mourners to cry 'Yuk!' in response. But no one made a sound, apart from my brother, who was sobbing loudly. He'd held back his tears for a week, and could contain himself no longer. Ben was sitting on my right, Natalie on my left.

As part of the service, the vicar had agreed to play Gina's favourite song over the address system. It was 'Miss You Nights', by her hero, the lovely Cliff. This made everyone cry, apart from the vicar, and Natalie, who sat rigidly to attention, staring straight ahead, a beautiful stoic in her desolation.

Ben kept wiping his snotty nose on his sleeve. Without thinking, I reached into my jacket, extracted a handkerchief, then passed it to Ben. Only it wasn't a handkerchief. For a moment, the vicar stopped nodding and humming along to Cliff to stare, open-mouthed, at the sight of my brother blowing his nose on a pair of blue silk knickers.

I hadn't wanted any kind of social gathering after the funeral. I'd always considered it idiotic that bereaved people should be expected to feed their guests. It should be the other way round: the bastards who've taken the trouble to turn up should be feeding the bereaved.

But Natalie had taken the liberty of hiring the services of a friend from the sisterhood who ran a wholefood catering business called Lesbeans. She was a separatist caterer, who normally catered for women only. But because she was Natalie's friend, and in view of the tragic circumstances, she'd agreed to make an exception, on condition that she didn't have to fraternize with any penis-owners. By the time we had all trudged in from the snow, the Lesbean had been and gone, and Natalie's kitchen table was laden with organic wine and food-free pies.

I started drinking as soon as I got back. Not organic wine, but some Boddington's Bitter that Ben had supplied. Inebriation was my only way of dealing with the endless line of acquaintances that trooped up to ask how I was feeling. What was I expected to say? That I'd experienced mild depression during the service, but that the sight of the coffin disappearing into the oven had perked me up enormously?

I wanted to be left alone. But no one seemed to think it was safe to leave me alone. Charles and Vaughan were present to represent my men's group. Gordon had been unable to attend because he'd been due in court, and Malcolm had stayed at home because he found funerals depressing. Charles seemed to think that it was necessary to tell me a funny story.

This is what he told me. At college, Charles and the student he roomed with used to have shitting contests. They lived three floors above street level. At night it was their custom to stick their arses out of the window of their room and shit on to the pavement below. The object of the exercise was common assault. The shitter whose turd hit an innocent bystander was the winner.

They tried for months, often shitting on the pavement, sometimes shitting on cars, but not once succeeding in hitting a passer-by. One night, while they were entertaining two girlfriends, the women decided to go out to buy some wine. In their absence, Charles and his friend held another shitting contest. They sat on the window sill, their bare arses exposed to the night air, and waited for someone to walk under the window. Eventually, hearing footsteps below, Charles prepared to release a turd.

At that moment, the door to his room opened, and the girlfriends walked in, carrying a bottle. In horror, Charles leapt off the sill and into the room. And a long brown turd dropped out of his arse, rolled across the carpet and came to rest at the feet of his girlfriend. Neither Charles nor his room-mate saw either of those women again.

By the time Charles had finished this story, he and Vaughan were laughing so much that they ached. I didn't laugh once. I didn't think the story was funny at all. I still don't.

I excused myself, and, like Captain Oates, slipped out alone into the snow. I was shivering in the drive-way when a shiny new Daimler Double-Six pulled up outside the house. The automatic window whizzed down, and a round, red face appeared.

'Hiya, mate!'

I couldn't believe it. It was Bomber.

He parked the car and walked over to me, dressed in an expensive dark pin-stripe suit. But the dashing effect created by the suit was marred somewhat by the muddy wellington boots that he was wearing on his feet.

His face was sober and sad. He strode over, gave me a bear-hug, and said, 'Sorry I'm late, mate. I meant to go to the church, but the car wouldn't start.'

'I can't believe you're here. You amaze me, John.'

I intended this as an insult, but he took it as a compliment.

'Why? You're a mate, aren't you?' He slapped me on the shoulder, adding, 'My mum saw it advertised in the *Manchester Evening News*.'

I sneered. 'I don't think "advertised" is quite the right word, is it?'

Flustered, he said, 'You know ... on the Deaths page. I'm sorry, pal. I'm fucked off about it all, honest I am.'

I found it difficult to be angry with someone so ignorant. But I had to try. 'Bomber, don't you think you're showing remarkable bad taste, even for someone as remarkably tasteless as you?'

Misunderstanding, he glanced down at his wellingtons. 'Sorry. I didn't want to get me trousers wet.'

He had no idea what I was getting at. No idea at all. I couldn't leave him standing out in the cold, so I invited him into the house. Natalie was by the door, talking to Ariadne, who had travelled up from London for the day. As she listened to Nat, Ariadne wore the familiar glazed expression that she reserved for people with large vocabularies. I introduced them both to Bomber, gritting my teeth as I waited for him to make some ribald remark about Natalie's pregnancy, or Ariadne's leathery neck. But he merely smiled politely and shook their hands.

I saw Ben talking to my dad in the living room, so judged it safe to lead Bomber into the kitchen. He wasn't hungry, so I gave him some organic wine. He asked what had happened to Gina, and I told him, omitting any mention of Josephine. He'd always been a big-mouth, so I braced myself, expecting some tactless reference to Jo and her talent for blow-jobs. But he was gentle and subdued, and said nothing tasteless or filthy, which left him with very little to say. That suited me fine.

Then Ben walked up to me, and, pointing at Bomber, yelled, 'Who let that bastard in?'

Ben's eyes were bloodshot. He was pissed. Bomber chuckled, trying to turn it into a joke. But Ben wasn't joking. He squared up to Bomber, shouting, 'I know all about you, you fucking bastard!'

'Shut up, Ben,' I said. 'It's a funeral, for God's sake!'

But he wasn't listening to me. He drew back his arm, and aimed a ridiculously telegraphed blow at Bomber's face. Bomber saw it coming, made no attempt to protect himself, merely grunted as my brother's palm connected with his head. Bomber simply stood there, looking sad and disappointed, a red mark appearing on his left cheek.

Then Ben yanked Bomber up by the lapels and hurled

him at the kitchen table. Bomber held on to Ben as he fell, and the pair of them crashed on to the table, squashing several cakes and a cream-free trifle. The table overturned, scattering food everywhere, and tipping Bomber and Ben on to the floor. They rolled about, wriggling and swearing, as out-of-place as two wrestlers at a funeral. Which, of course, is exactly what they were. Hearing the commotion, my mother ran up to them and started beating Ben on the arse with a large wooden spoon.

She'd always thought of Ben as a naughty boy, and this ultimate proof of his naughtiness sent her completely out of control. My father tried to restrain her, slipped on some fruit salad, and both my parents joined Ben and Bomber on the floor. Then Charles and Vaughan joined forces to unravel the threshing bodies, but also slipped and fell on to the lino. It was a deeply degrading spectacle. Gina would have pissed herself laughing.

As soon as Ben was upright, Rachel dragged him away, showing a physical strength surprising in one so religious. In reply to her demand for an explanation, we heard him shouting, 'What's it about? He knows what it's about, the fat bastard!'

Bomber was badly shaken. He hadn't anticipated a scuffle and had only fought to protect his honour. Using kitchen towels, Natalie and I wiped the trifle off his head, and out of his ears. I gave him a consoling can of beer from the fridge, without mentioning that it was beer that his attacker had paid for.

Natalie questioned us. 'What was it about? It must have been about something.'

Bomber was genuinely mystified. He shook his head, dazed. 'I stole the pump off his bike when we were kids. I can't think what else it could be.'

*

It was the night of the day of the funeral. Natalie and I were finally alone. We were huddled together on the sofa, drinking hot chocolate. It had been a long day, and we were preparing for bed.

Natalie suddenly said, 'What was wrong with Ben, Guy?'

'I don't know, Nat,' I said. 'I think he was just upset.'

She stirred her chocolate reflectively. 'He's got a serious aggression problem, your brother.'

'He's all right,' I argued. 'He never hits women or children.'

'Oh. So that makes it all right, does it?'

'No. But he's not a bully. He only hits people who are bigger than him.'

'That's not difficult, is it? Most people are bigger than your brother.' We sighed in unison. She said, 'Anyway, what was he fighting about this time?'

'Nothing,' I said. 'He was just upset.'

'I thought it might have had something to do with Gina.'

'I dare say it did,' I answered smoothly. 'We're all upset because of Gina.'

'I didn't mean that.'

'So what did you mean?'

'I don't know. You tell me, Guy.'

'How can *I* tell you what *you* mean, Nat? I don't even know what you're talking about.'

She was quiet for a few seconds. When she spoke again, her voice had chilled by several degrees.

'Well, he wasn't upset about a fucking bicycle pump, was he?'

I began to feel scared. 'What makes you think it was about Gina? Bomber and Gina didn't know each other. They never met.'

She stared at me, in the same sulky way that little kids stare at people when they haven't yet learned the value of hypocrisy.

114

Having finished my chocolate, I rose to my feet. I didn't like the direction the conversation was taking. 'Really, Natalie,' I insisted. 'I'm sure it wasn't about anything. Ben just got upset.'

Her eyes seemed to grow darker and wider as they explored my face. Half-nodding, she sipped her drink and let the matter drop. I kissed her goodnight, but she didn't kiss me back. She knew that I'd lied to her.

The Ninth Secret

For the next month I retreated from the world, with the world's blessing. Apart from attending Natalie's final ante-natal classes, I rarely left the house. Ariadne Marryat-Legh gave me three months leave with pay. I was only a freelance contributor, so the old nag was actually treating me with exceptional kindness.

Natalie didn't pursue the matter of Ben and Bomber's fight. In those first weeks after the funeral, a strange calm descended upon her. There was no mistaking the love she felt for Gina, or the loneliness she was left with. Yet since Gina's death, I had not seen her shed a single tear.

To me, she was sweetness itself, and, like everyone else, seemed to regard me with pity and awe. People were touched by my loss because Gina had been young and beautiful. Had she been old, or young but fat, or old, fat and drunk like her mother, her loss would have seemed sad but somehow ordinary. Her youthful loveliness lent her death greater meaning, not just to neighbours and distant relations, but to Natalie and me, who ought to have known better, and would have treasured Gina at any age, and at any weight.

Natalie erected a shrine to Gina, in a corner of my room. It contained sea-shells and candles, incense and story-books, ribbons, flowers and dolls. At its heart lay our framed wedding photograph, bordered by pictures of Rose with her girls when they were children. There was even a photo of

Gina's idol, Cliff Richard. When the shrine was finished, Natalie called me in.

This was to be our service for Gina, not like the church service, which had been a mere formality, but a private farewell from two people who had truly loved her. Together, we lit the candles. I stood beside Natalie while she took out her violin and, without sheet music, played 'The Lark Ascending' by Vaughan Williams. She played beautifully, with a sweetness that defied all description, the notes swirling upwards towards heaven. Then, abruptly, she stopped playing and gasped.

A startled look crossed her face. Then she laughed and, lowering the violin, held her right hand over the mound in her maternity dress. 'The baby's kicking,' she said.

She invited me to touch her belly, and then clasped her hand over mine. Her belly felt hard and tight, like the skin of a drum. I felt a dull ripple inside her.

'Shit,' I said. 'I hope he's not going to be a footballer. I hate football.'

'Who says it's going to be a boy?' she said.

Then, without warning, she began to cry. Gently, I took the violin and bow away from her and laid them on my bed. Then I held her close, while she literally howled with grief, and our unborn child wriggled and kicked inside her.

Malcolm was jealous.

It was my first men's group meeting for eight months, and I had a lot to talk about. I'd fucked a porn model, my wife had died, and her sister was about to give birth to my child. Nothing had happened to Malcolm at all. All he could say was the same thing that he said every month, which was, 'As you know, I've been splitting up from my partner. It's been a painful time for me, and this group has saved my life. Thank you for your support.'

This month, however, none of us thanked him back. A

little savagely, Charles said, 'Tell me, Mal. Is this the same partner you've been breaking up from for the past two years?'

Malcolm turned white. His normal colour was a kind of puky brownish-pink. We were sitting in the living room of Natalie's house. It was a Sunday afternoon, and Natalie had gone out to a recording studio in Didsbury. She liked to earn extra money by playing the odd session.

'What do you mean?' said Malcolm.

Charles smiled wolfishly. 'I mean, how can you possibly have been splitting up from the same woman for two years? Surely, you've actually *split* by now? Isn't it about time you employed the past participle?'

'That's right,' said Gordon. 'I thought your partner was living with someone else?'

'They hardly live together,' snapped Malcolm testily. 'They're married.'

Charles laughed. 'Well, how can you still be splitting up, then, you silly sod?'

Malcolm bit his upper lip. 'It's an on-going process.' Charles jeered. Vaughan frowned. 'No. No. Malcolm has a point, there. Has anyone read a book called *Love and Let Love*? No? It's by this amazing man called Sammy Kumquat.'

The rest of us sulked, knowing full well that the only amazing thing about Sammy Kumquat would be his amazingly stupid name. But Vaughan went on to say, 'He was born with only one leg, and ran away from home when he was six . . .'

'Shouldn't that be "hopped" away from home?' interrupted Charles.

'Shut up, Charles. And listen. You might learn something. He ran away from home and joined a circus. He became an acrobat. Then, at the age of thirteen, he went blind. He fell off a tight-rope.'

118

'What was he doing on a tight-rope when he was blind?' asked Charles.

'He could see before he fell,' hissed Vaughan between clenched teeth. 'It was the fall that made him blind.'

I said, 'Just a minute. He only had one leg. How do you walk a tight-rope with one leg?'

'Ah!' said Vaughan, raising his forefinger significantly. 'That's another amazing thing about Kumquat. He used to walk the tight-rope on his *hands*.'

With a disdainful little sniff, Charles said, 'It's not really that amazing, is it? If he'd been any good at walking a tight-rope on his hands, he wouldn't have fallen off.'

'Well, Charles, I'll bet you couldn't walk a tight-rope on your hands *or* your feet.'

'No,' admitted Charles. 'But I could fall off.'

Gordon sighed. Vaughan's flair for infinite digression was beginning to grate on him. 'Vaughan, if there's a point to this story, would you mind getting to it?'

Vaughan paused to give Gordon a look of hurt surprise. Then he said, 'OK. The central theme running through *Love and Let Love* is the idea that relationships are not determined by beginnings and ends, and that even if you haven't spoken to a person for twenty years, or even if that person is dead, it still counts as a relationship.'

'Bollocks,' said Charles.

Vaughan continued, 'And another thing, Charles. I don't think that calling Malcolm a "silly sod" is very helpful.'

'It helps me,' said Charles.

'And me,' said Gordon. Then he and Charles fell about laughing.

Malcolm glared at them emotionally. 'I see. It's "get Malcolm" time again, is it?'

The laughter intensified. Piously, I said, 'No. Come on. Vaughan's right. If we're going to resort to petty insults, we might as well give up.'

Malcolm thanked me, unaware that my intervention had been motivated by self-interest. I knew that if the barracking continued, Malcolm would burst into tears. Then the group would have to build a wall of love around him and as I've said before, Malcolm had a bit of a hygiene problem.

Charles took out a cigarette and contemplated it, as if he was unsure whether to smoke it or shove it up Vaughan's arse.

'No smoking in this house, Charles,' I reminded him.

'Of course,' he said. 'Sorry.' He slotted the cigarette back into its packet.

Vaughan made an announcement: 'I think Malcolm wants to say something.'

Malcolm nodded. 'Yes, I do. I want to say that I'm feeling frightened. Yes, I think "frightened" is the right word. I feel that all of you are against me. Except Vaughan and Guy.'

Charles and Gordon were trying not to laugh.

Vaughan said, 'Would anyone care to comment on what Malcolm has just said?'

'Yes,' said Gordon. 'I would. I'd like to comment.'

The room went silent. Although Gordon was well-liked, and envied for his great big dick, he was essentially a lazy, apathetic bastard. Most of the time, he could barely find the energy to scratch his arse, let alone initiate a conversation. So we were eager to hear what he had to say. (All right: perhaps 'eager' is putting it a bit strong. Let's just say we were moderately curious.)

Gordon said, 'I *have* been feeling, well, a bit impatient with you, Malcolm.'

'Thank you for telling me,' said Malcolm, without sounding at all grateful.

'And I've been feeling annoyed with *you*, Vaughan, and *you*, Charles. Because what has happened to Guy has been devastating. I mean that. Truly *devastating*.'

They hung their heads in humble acknowledgement.

120

'His life has been torn apart! And what do we do? The same as we always do! Malcolm whinges. No, I'm sorry Malcolm, but it's true. You whinge. Vaughan shows off about the bloody awful books he's read. Charles makes bad jokes. It's just not good enough.'

'I don't make bad jokes,' contended Charles. 'You were pissing yourself at my jokes five minutes ago.'

'I know,' said Gordon. 'But I didn't like myself while I was doing it.'

Vaughan nodded. 'So let's get this straight, Gordon. You think we should be talking about Guy, do you?'

Gordon said, 'Well, yes. I think he needs our support.'

Vaughan looked at Charles. 'Well?'

Charles blinked innocently. 'Well what?'

'Nothing. I'm just waiting for you to say something rude,' explained Vaughan.

'Sticky bum-hairs.' Charles beamed. 'Is that rude enough for you? However, jesting apart, I agree with Gordon. I think we should be trying to help Guy.'

Vaughan smiled. 'We're all in agreement, then. OK, Guy. Tell us how you're feeling.'

Hesitantly, I told them that I couldn't help feeling that I'd murdered my wife by betraying her. I said that I suspected I was a fairly unpleasant person, and they scoffed at the very idea. Then I told them how much I loved Natalie, and longed to have sex with her, and they suddenly stopped scoffing. I sensed that the notion of my unpleasantness was suddenly not as risible as it had been a moment before. No one knew what to say. Apart from Vaughan.

'So you feel guilty because you think you've killed your wife, but you still want to have sexual intercourse with her sister?' he said, with unexpected harshness.

'Yes,' I agreed. 'But I only want to have sex with her because I love her.'

'Quite sure about that, are we? Who's running this show,

121

Guy: "Mr Heart" or "Mr Penis"? Because, I must say, it doesn't sound as if you're exactly racked by remorse.'

'Judgemental,' chirped Malcolm. 'Vaughan's being judgemental.'

'No,' I said. 'Vaughan's right. He's right. I probably am a bastard. I've turned it over and over in my mind, and the conclusion I always reach is that I'm a selfish bastard.'

'I wouldn't go that far,' said Vaughan. 'But I think you should try thinking *before* you act, rather than after.'

Charles suddenly said, 'Vaughan, you read a lot. Have you come across a book called *I Tell the Truth and You Spit on Me?*'

Taken aback, Vaughan said, 'Er, no. I mean, yes. I mean I haven't read it. But I've heard of it.'

'That's funny,' said Charles, 'because it doesn't exist.'

Everyone, with the inevitable exception of Vaughan, rocked with laughter. Showing the strain, Vaughan said, 'Yes, yes. Very funny.'

'It's a book I've made up,' said Charles. 'It's a book about Guy, and people like him, who trust others with the truth and are despised for it. The sequel is a book about you. It's called *I'm a Sanctimonious Bearded Prick.*'

To his credit, Vaughan apologized. 'All right. Fair enough. Guy . . . everyone. I'm sorry. Maybe I *am* finding what Guy's got to say hard to deal with.'

'But that's your problem, not his,' opined Malcolm.

'Yes,' conceded Vaughan. 'It *is* my problem. And I'll have to work through it. Perhaps Guy would like me to leave the room for a while?'

'Yes,' I said. 'Bugger off.'

Vaughan looked very downhearted. 'Really? You really want me to go?'

'No,' I said. 'I'm joking.'

Malcolm had an idea. 'I think we should all hold hands.'

The other group members agreed. All five of us linked

hands. Unfortunately, I was sandwiched between Gordon and Malcolm. Holding Malcolm's hand was like squeezing a kipper that had been cooked in oil and left to go cold.

Gordon, who was excelling himself today, spoke again. 'So, Guy, you're living with a woman who's about to have your baby. And you love her, but can't tell her?'

'That's about the size of it,' I said.

'Why can't you tell her?'

'Because it might destroy everything,' I said.

'What do you mean by "everything"?' asked Malcolm.

'Well,' I answered, 'I mean that things are OK as they are. Really. For the time being, anyway.'

Charles said, 'I have to admit, she's a highly fuckable piece.' Malcolm sighed in disapproval, and Charles apologized. 'Sorry. I mean she's a fuckable *woman*.'

Still addressing me, Gordon said, 'Yes, Guy, but it won't make you happy, will it? Living with someone you love, but not being able to express your love openly? It sounds like torture, to me. You're not a masochist, by any chance?'

'No,' I stressed. 'No, I'm not.'

'I think you should tell her the truth,' said Malcolm.

'So do I,' added Gordon.

I was taken aback. This unusual course of action had not occurred to me. 'What? Tell her I love her, you mean?'

'Tell her everything you've told us. Why not?' said Vaughan.

'She'd never speak to me again.'

'You don't *know* that.'

'No,' I said. 'But I'm not willing to risk it.'

Vaughan creased up his face as if my dilemma was causing him pain. 'You've told a lot of lies, Guy. But I don't think lying has ever made you particularly happy. Would you agree with that assessment?'

'I wouldn't disagree,' I replied cautiously.

'I would,' said Charles. 'I don't hold with all this

"honesty" rubbish. Men and women talk to each other too much as it is.'

'He doesn't mean that,' commented Malcolm. 'He's just saying that to upset me.'

Charles said 'No. I really think that men make themselves very unhappy by talking to women.'

'What do you expect us to do instead?' asked Malcolm.

'Hide.'

We all laughed. Charles pretended not to see the joke.

'No, I'm perfectly serious. When a man sees a sexy lady approaching, he should find a good hiding place and stay there until it's safe to come out. It'd save a great deal of unhappiness.'

Malcolm made his usual mistake of taking Charles seriously. 'Firstly, both the terms "sexy" and "lady" are unworthy of a man of your intelligence. And, more importantly, if everyone felt as you do, the human race would die out.'

Charles nodded. 'Exactly,' he said. 'Bloody good job.'

'But Charles,' said Malcolm.

'But Malcolm,' said Charles.

Vaughan said, 'Anyway, Charles, we're not suggesting that Guy spends the rest of his life talking to Natalie. We just think he should be honest with her at the outset of their relationship. It's up to him whether he talks to her later on. But remember that so far their relationship has remained platonic. To use tabloid terminology, they are "just good friends" who haven't yet had their first date. I imagine that even *you*, Charles, would talk to a woman on a first date.'

Charles shuddered slightly. 'Good Lord, no.'

Gordon said, 'I think you'd feel better, Guy, if you set the record straight with Natalie. Tell her as much as you feel you can, without hurting her, of course.'

'That's right,' said Vaughan. 'There's always a middle

way. Let's not forget what *I Love You if You Love Me* has to teach us about honesty.'

'Oh, *do* fuck off,' said Charles.

Gordon held my hand up as if I'd just won a boxing bout. 'I don't think you're risking much, Guy. She obviously already fancies you.'

Freeing my arm, I said, 'Would you testify to that in a court of law?'

'Yesss . . . It's obvious, man. Having showers in front of you, running about with no knickers on.'

'That doesn't mean anything,' I said. 'Women like to walk about without knickers.'

'My wife doesn't,' said Gordon. As an afterthought, he added, 'Thank God.'

'Gordon!' hissed Malcolm. 'That is *so* sexist!'

Gordon jeered. 'Well . . . Natalie is clearly *begging* for it. Must be. So why else would she be showing Guy all she's got? Come on, Guy. Be a man. Tell her how you feel. She'll probably tear your bloody clothes off.'

'I agree,' said Vaughan, red-faced. 'In fact, to save time, why not tell her while you're already naked?'

'Vaughan!' scolded Malcolm.

'Come on. How many of us think Guy should own up?' demanded Gordon.

Without hesitation, Vaughan and Gordon thrust their arms into the air. Reluctantly, Malcolm followed their example. Charles shook his head gloomily.

Vaughan gave me a patronizing smile. Patronizing smiles were his speciality. 'Looks like the "ayes" have it, Guy. Better tell her. Tell her you fancy the pants off her.'

'They're already off,' Charles reminded him.

I was about to argue when Malcolm confessed to a growing feeling of isolation. 'I'm getting the impression that no one is remotely interested in me today,' he complained.

With some weariness, Vaughan suggested that we should restore Malcolm's faith in the group by playing the 'trust game'. Malcolm thought this was worth a try. We all stood up and formed a circle, with Malcolm in the centre. Malcolm closed his eyes, and allowed his entire body to go limp. As he flopped, I caught him and tossed him over to another member of the group. Wherever he fell, there was someone waiting to support him.

After a few minutes of this, he opened his eyes, visibly rejuvenated. 'Thank you,' he announced. 'You've made me feel truly valued.'

We broke for coffee. Vaughan took out a note-book and pen and asked each of us to supply him with a cheque. He'd booked a house in Devon, where we were all destined to spend a weekend in July. We'd been talking about such a trip for the last two years, without suspecting that it would ever materialize. But Vaughan had made the final arrangements without consulting us, and none of us possessed the courage or the energy to back out. Our trip was intended to provide forty-eight hours of intensive discussion and self-discovery.

'Lucky for you that the trip's come at this time, Guy,' enthused Vaughan, as he wrote out a receipt for my cheque. 'You'll have a whole weekend to engage with your problems. And won't the baby have been born by then?'

I nodded.

'Thought so.' He grinned, rubbing his hands together. 'You can tell us all about your first impressions of fatherhood. It'll be a chance for the group to get really close.'

Gordon left early to pick his son up from cub camp, and gave Vaughan a lift home. Charles drank some coffee, then mounted the bicycle he had purchased in an effort to improve his physical fitness and cycled away with a fag hanging from his mouth. Malcolm stayed an extra fifteen minutes, until his bus was due, drank a second cup of coffee and almost wept.

He almost wept because I had temporarily ousted him from his position as the group's resident wreck. But he couldn't quite allow himself to succumb to his usual convulsions of grief, knowing that there would be other group meetings and, therefore, further opportunities for riotous self-pity, and that long after my personal tragedy was forgotten, the tragedy of Malcolm being Malcolm would continue. Malcolm didn't expect much from life, but he was unfailingly optimistic about his own prospects for future unhappiness.

When he'd gone, I opened all the windows to let out his unmistakable aroma: a blend of brussel sprouts and unwashed socks. Then I checked the answer-machine for messages. There had been two calls. I played back the tape and heard a squeaky woman's voice say, 'Guy, it's me. I mean, it's me, Josephine. I've not heard from yer for ages, so I hope you've got my phone number. See you later.'

A chill passed through me. Then I remembered that, to Londoners, the phrase 'See you later' can mean anything from 'See you next week' to 'See you before one of us dies'. I heard a posse of peeps, and then the same childish voice, saying, 'Oh, yeah, yeah, I nearly forgot. I never give yer me number. It's . . . it's . . . what is it? Oh shit. Sorry. Sorry. I'll ring back when I remember . . .'

Out in the street, someone laughed.

I glanced through the window and saw Natalie getting out of a powder-blue Porsche. I was surprised, because I wouldn't normally have associated Natalie with such a vulgar mode of transport. A bespectacled bearded man left the car and handed her violin case to her. He looked a bit like Rob Mitchell, a man who read the local news on television.

They exchanged a few pleasantries, then the bearded

bastard climbed into his vulgar mode of transport and drove away. Before Natalie had time to enter the house, I wrenched the cassette out of the answer-machine and pocketed it. There was every possibility that Josephine would ring again to give me her telephone number: a number, incidentally, that was already listed in my address book under 'Computer Repairs'.

'You're early,' I said to Natalie, kissing her and relieving her of the violin case.

'It was an easy session. It only took two takes.'

She kicked off her sandals and flopped sideways on to the sofa, with her bare feet resting on the wall. She had long, pretty feet and their nails were painted harlot-red. Her flowered maternity dress fell back around her waist, exposing her white knickers and her lean brown legs. I felt a sudden stab of sexual jealousy.

I perched on the arm of the sofa. 'Who gave you the lift?' I tried to make the enquiry casual, but it came out sounding like a challenge.

She grinned, showing perfectly white and even teeth. 'Didn't you recognize him?'

'It looked like that twat who reads the news.'

She giggled. 'It *was*. It *was* that twat who reads the news. Rob Mitchell. He was sitting in on the session.'

'Why?'

'The band I was playing for . . . The Keepers . . . have just signed to his record label.'

Rob Mitchell was an announcer from *Northern Eye*, a local TV news programme. Mitchell was desperate to be seen as an artist, rather than a man who merely read out reports about 'higher bus fares for the North West'. So he had opened a club in Manchester called the Verandah and started up his own independent record label, Conveyor Belt. Mitchell saw himself as a kind of Andy Warhol with sex appeal – so many years ahead of the action that only time travellers could hope to catch up with him. But to unenlightened observers, Mitchell, with his beard, his tan, his fawn casual trousers and his open-necked south-sea island shirts, resembled an affluent middle-aged hairdresser on a night out in Benidorm.

'Is he as twatty as he looks?'

She started moving her feet up and down the wall. 'Not really. To be fair, he's quite nice. He was pretty impressed by my playing. He says he wants to be my patron.'

'Meaning he wants to go to bed with you.'

'I shouldn't think so,' she said. 'He's married. Besides, have you taken a good look at me lately?'

She meant that she was far too pregnant to be sexually attractive. Not realizing that I would have sold my soul, there and then, to have her sitting on my face.

'What does a patron do?'

'Well,' she mused. 'Traditionally, a patron gives an artist money, clothes, somewhere to live.'

'That's funny,' I said. 'Isn't that also what rich husbands traditionally give to their mistresses?'

She smiled – a slow, relaxed Natalie smile. 'Don't worry, Guy. I can look after myself.'

A fortnight before the baby was due, I went round to visit my mum and dad. A friend of theirs had donated a cot for the baby, and left it in their garage. Dad decided that it was my job to collect the cot and take it to Natalie. When I arrived, I realized that the only reason that my parents hadn't ferried the cot to Shepley Drive themselves was that they wanted to talk to me alone.

As the three of us sat together, sipping tea, Mum said, without preamble, 'Now, what about this baby, Guy?'

'What about it?' I answered queasily, wondering whether my big brother had been opening his big mouth.

'Well, we don't know anything about it,' explained Dad.

'I mean, who's the father? Has Natalie got a young man or not? Is she even courting?'

To Mum and Dad, boyfriends and girlfriends had always been 'young men' and 'young ladies', and everything that people from these two categories did together prior to marriage, including kissing, fondling and rampant shafting, was known as 'courting'.

'No,' I said. 'She hasn't got a boyfriend.'

They exchanged gloomy glances. Mum said, 'Well, how's she going to cope with a kiddy on her own?'

'She won't be on her own,' I said, trying to sound encouraging. 'She'll have my help. From now on, anything I earn, I share with Natalie.'

At this news, Mum seemed to start slightly in her chair. Or maybe it was just wind. 'But has it occurred to you, lad, that as long as you're both together in that house, people will think something funny's going on?'

'People? What people?' I sneered. 'Do you mean you and Dad?'

'No,' interjected Dad. 'Your mother doesn't mean anything. It's just that, well, you living there, son, and Natalie about to have a baby. It looks bad, really.'

'You think so, do you?'

'I *do* think so,' said Dad.

'Would it look bad if Gina was still alive?' I asked him.

He pulled a face, as if he'd tasted something sour. It still pained him to admit that Gina was dead. 'No. Of course not. That'd be completely different.'

'No, it wouldn't. I'd be living with my wife and my wife's pregnant sister. But my relationship with Natalie would be the same as it's always been.'

They were silent for a while. Finally, Mum said, 'We don't want an argument. We're only asking.'

'And I'm only telling you.'

She offered me a piece of shortbread. I accepted. She

watched me eat it, then said, 'What bothers *me* is: who's going to be there when the little one's born?'

'I am,' I said.

Alarm made them jerk upright in their seats. 'Now, that *would* be stupid,' declared Dad. 'That's something that only fathers do.'

Unfairly, I said 'You didn't do it.'

'They didn't allow it, in our day,' he responded, looking wounded. 'I've only ever seen Ben's hamsters being born.'

Mum said, 'I was wondering if Natalie wanted *me* to be there.'

I nearly laughed, but stopped myself just in time. 'You?' I said.

To convey an impression of sincerity, Mum outstretched her arms, exposing the palms of her hands. It was a gesture she'd picked up from watching old Al Jolson films. 'Why not? I've been through it all myself, you know. And it seems a shame for Natalie, with no mother or husband, all alone in a great big hospickal.'

(Don't ask me why, but to Mum, sick people went to 'hospickal', water was boiled in a 'keckle' and men who wore kilts came from 'Scockland'.)

'She won't necessarily be alone, Mum,' I argued. 'There might even be a few doctors and nurses around.'

Tersely, Dad said, 'You know what your mother means.'

As gently as I could, I said, 'Thanks for offering, Mum. But Natalie wants me to be there. I know she'd have preferred Gina, but Gina's not here any more. I'm all Natalie's got now, and I've made up my mind to look after her.'

Natalie had a birth-plan. The plan was as follows: to give birth to a baby, with as little fuss and as little medication as possible. It was my job to ensure that this modest aim was carried out. Natalie also expected me to prevent the hospital staff from sticking needles in her or the baby during labour, and to help her into any childbearing position she wanted to try. If any nurse or midwife tried to interfere with our birth-plan, without reasonable cause, it was my solemn duty to punch them in the face.

The baby was born at Stepping Hill Hospital, where Rose had died. Our midwife was a sanguine West Indian woman called Melvis. She had no objections to our birth-plan, which was fortunate, because punching her in the face would have been a perilous undertaking. She was about six foot two, with breasts like two nuclear warheads and forearms like sides of beef.

The labour started at four in the morning on 15 May and lasted for twelve and a quarter hours. While she grunted, sweated and screamed, Natalie's favourite Bach tapes played on a ghetto-blaster. Johann Sebastian was part of the birth-plan, too. Melvis assumed that I was Natalie's partner, and neither Natalie nor I contradicted her.

While she went about her business, Melvis made jokes about me for Natalie's benefit. She seemed to think that all men were buffoons. As if to prove her right, I almost missed the baby's arrival. While the baby's head was 'crowning', I was strolling around the hospital car-park, inhaling the evening air and eating biscuits. I was missing Gina and felt so sad that I ate a whole packet of Jaffa Cakes. When I returned to the delivery room, chocolate smeared around my mouth, Melvis said, 'Just like a man. He go stuffing his face when there's work to be done.'

Then Melvis laughed and, grabbing my arm roughly, yanked me over to gaze at the miracle taking place between Natalie's legs. I looked on, in open-mouthed wonder. This would have been the best view I'd ever had of Natalie's cunt. But, unfortunately, it had a baby's head sticking out of it.

132

The Final Secret

It was a boy.

He was born with a head full of dark tufty hair and a penis that squirted real water. I had expected to feel nothing more than mild affection for the mite, but in fact he amazed me. He looked like a perfect cross between Natalie and me; perfect in the sense that he looked more like her than me. And he had a good pair of bollocks on him. Just like his mother.

While he'd been growing inside her, my only feeling with regard to my coming heir had been smug satisfaction; I'd viewed the baby as a contract signed in blood by its mother and me, pledging us to eternal involvement in each other's lives.

But at the sight of him, with his exquisitely sculptured miniature finger-nails and his red, screwed-up, bawling face, I fell prey to an unexpected flood of emotion.

Love without desire.

Natalie walked everywhere with him in her arms, half-exhausted, half-delirious with dreamy bliss. She toyed with the idea of calling him John, until I pointed out that this was a name that prostitutes used to describe their clients. I suggested Gene, after her sister, but she said that this made him sound like part of a chromosome. So we settled on Eric, after Natalie's Uncle Eric, who had given Natalie her first violin. But we spelt it 'Erik', so that when he grew up, girls would still fancy him.

I bought a video-camera, and then, like any doting

working-class thicko, began to film my offspring. I filmed Natalie feeding Erik, and Erik in close-up, looking like a wrinkled prune. Then Natalie filmed me and Erik together, early in the morning, when both of us looked like wrinkled prunes.

Erik had a trick. When he was lying on his back, he could piss three feet into the air. He pissed in my face twice during his first week of life, while I was trying to change his nappy. He never pissed on Natalie, only on me.

I wonder if he knew.

Watching her feeding him, in the living room at 13 Shepley Drive, I was overcome by searing love for that happy mother and the greedy little bastard at her breast. A procession of well-wishers marched through the house to inspect the latest drain on the planet's resources. While my parents held him, staring into his unfocused eyes, and crediting him with intellectual attributes that he did not yet possess, I was indeed grateful that he resembled his mother rather than his father.

The only people who did not enter the house were Natalie's feminist friends. A trio of them turned up one day, riding in a white van with 'Lesbeans' written on the side. The van was driven by Lesley Bean herself: a thin woman with a long, gaunt Irish Catholic face. To my horror, she was wearing large white football shorts that ballooned over her pale, sinewy legs. She was accompanied by two other women with brutal hair-cuts and huge, wandering arses.

When Natalie saw them, she waved joyously and took the baby out for inspection. The four women stood out in the drive, passing the baby around and making soppy noises for over an hour. Natalie came into the house, made some coffee and took it out to them on a tray. It started to drizzle. The visitors spent the next thirty minutes saying farewell, before climbing into their van and trundling away.

When Natalie entered the house, I said, 'It was raining. Why didn't you bring them in?'

She was in the kitchen, dabbing at Erik's damp brow with a towel. 'You were here,' she said simply.

'I wouldn't have minded.'

'No,' she said. 'But they'd have minded. They're separatists, Guy. They don't associate with men. Full stop.'

'I still don't see why they couldn't have come into the house. Or do buildings have genders, too?'

She passed the baby to me, perhaps meaning to pacify me. 'But you live here, Guy. You're a man.'

I was annoyed. A newborn baby had been left out in the rain because a group of women had principles. 'So what? I don't spunk up all over the walls, do I? I don't wear T-shirts with "suck my cock" printed on them. Anyway, why didn't they want to be separate from Erik? He's a man, isn't he? Or were they only holding him because he hasn't raped anyone yet?'

She eyed me coolly, then snatched the baby back. She walked over to the door, with Erik's head lolling on her shoulder. Then she turned to me and said, 'Guy, don't *ever* let me hear you talk like that again.'

I made Erik my confidant. I held long conversations with him, in Natalie's absence. He was a good listener. When he wasn't crying, he looked so detached, composed and wise. Admittedly, there wasn't much wisdom in the way he crapped his nappy, or pissed in my eye. But I'd swear to God that my son understood me. Sometimes, I thought I could see Gina in his eyes, loving me from beyond the urn. Loving, not judging. But perhaps we only ever see what we want to see.

'It's getting worse, mate,' I told him.

Two days had passed since those dreadful dykes had tried

to drown him. Natalie was downstairs, absorbed in her nightly violin practice. She was playing something irritating by Vivaldi. I was in the bathroom, bathing Erik in the wash-basin.

'It's not about lust any more,' I told him. 'It's turning into that sickly butterflies feeling you get when you're thirteen years old. Except that you don't know about that feeling yet, Erik. But you will. You will.'

He gurgled reflectively. I was trying to wash his hair. His head felt like a small, warm coconut.

'I go all shaky when I'm near her. Does she make you feel like that? Eh? Does she?'

His response was non-committal.

'When you first love someone, it's difficult to tell them. But eventually, you reach the stage where it's harder *not* to tell them. That's the stage I'm at now. I need your advice, Erik. I want to tell her. But what'll happen if I do?'

He didn't answer. I rinsed his head. 'I'm in a right fucking mess, mate. What'll happen if I tell her?'

Glancing down at my son's penis, I saw that it was standing to attention, an exact erect replica of his daddy's reproductive organ. Only bigger. I took this as a sign that being truthful with Natalie would result in wild, abandoned physical love.

You will notice that I had invented my own personal system of oracular divination: dickomancy. Or in Erik's case, itty-bitty-dickomancy. The fact that I was prepared to base a life-changing decision on the involuntary movement of a baby boy's penis ought to give you some idea of my state of mind during those troubled weeks.

Afterwards, when the baby had been bedded down in his borrowed cot, Natalie and I settled down to watch tele-vision. She was keen to see a documentary about how the polluted waters of the Pacific were creating a new breed of mentally handicapped dolphins. Or, as the programme's

narrator put it, 'dolphins with special needs'. The programme set out to prove that, whereas dolphins of normal
intelligence could be trained to leap through a hoop, a
mentally handicapped dolphin would take one look at the
hoop, shrug and swim away. Some handicap.

I made myself a cheese and onion sandwich and joined
Nat on the sofa. She lay lengthways, with her head in my
lap. The film commenced with a school of perfectly normal
dolphins, frolicking underwater with a pair of scuba divers.
Wow. You should have seen those dolphins jumping
through hoops. You would have been as bored as I was.
The onion in my sandwich was a bit on the harsh side. My
eyes began to water.

Hearing me sniffing, Natalie raised herself to a kneeling
position and stared into my face. 'Hey,' she said, with gentle
concern. 'Guy.'

I was in tears because of an over-astringent edible bulb.
But Nat assumed that I'd been moved by the special needs
of the dolphins. She threw her arms around me. 'Don't cry,'
she counselled softly.

'I can't help it,' I said.

'You're right,' she said. 'There's nothing wrong with
being sensitive.' She kissed the tears away from my face.

'I love you,' I said.

She nodded calmly. 'I know. And I love you.'

'No,' I said. 'I *really* love you. Like Cathy and Heathcliff
. . . Tristan and Isolde . . . Little and Large.'

She reached for the TV remote control and plunged the
set into darkness. Her expression was grave and intense.
'Do you really mean that?' she said.

'Yes,' I said. 'I'm sorry. I love you, Nat. I can't help
myself.'

She nodded, as if she'd known this all along. 'I love you,
too,' she said.

Joyous heat surged through my loins. Her eyes had turned

all soft and moist. I thought I could spy a splendid fuck on the horizon. 'What? You mean it? You *really* love me?'

'Yes. I mean it.' She brushed my face with the tips of her fingers. It was like being touched by Christ, or one of his angels. She said, 'I think you're a lovely man. I've always thought so.'

I tried to kiss her, but she held me at bay. 'Don't,' she said. 'I want to ask you something.'

'What? What?'

'Who's Josephine?' she said.

I felt like a schoolboy who's had his trousers pulled down in front of the entire class. 'Why? She's just someone I know.'

Natalie noted my embarrassment. 'Who is she, Guy?'

'Why?' I blustered. 'Who've you been talking to?'

'I've been talking to Josephine,' explained Natalie. 'She phoned a few days ago, when you were out wheeling Erik round the block. She left her telephone number. And she gave me a message for you.'

'What message?'

'She says she's in this month's *Red Cheeks*. What's *Red Cheeks*, Guy?'

I felt myself blushing. 'I don't know. Isn't it a specialist magazine for people who suffer from social embarrassment?'

She shook her head. 'No, Guy. *Red Cheeks* is a magazine for unreconstructed men to masturbate to. It's full of photographs of women dressed as schoolgirls who are getting their bottoms spanked. It's a magazine that degrades women, and every man who reads it.'

'So's *Woman's Own*,' I said.

'Stop trying to evade the issue.'

'All right.' I lowered my eyes in penitence. 'Sorry.'

'Josephine had something to do with that fight on the day of the funeral, didn't she?'

'Yeah,' I answered. 'And I'll tell you all about it some day. I promise.'

She took my hand and pressed it urgently. 'No, Guy. You can't leave it at that. Not after what you've just said to me. If we're going to stay together, I want to know what's been going on. I want the truth.'

I was shivering. 'Promise you won't hate me?'

She squeezed my hand. 'Darling, how could I hate you?'

I was shocked. Natalie had never called me 'darling' before. It was that accursed word which gave me the courage to confess my sins. I told her everything, starting with the problems Gina and I had experienced in bed, moving on to my two hot saucy nights of kinky lust with Josephine, and ending on the blackest secret of all: the passion I'd always felt for Natalie. Natalie the strong, Natalie the cold, Natalie the stealer of souls.

She said nothing at all until I'd finished. Her face remained utterly blank. It was impossible to tell how my outpourings had affected her. Then she said 'And when you had sex with Josephine, did you use a condom?'

'Fucking right!' I replied. 'I'm not a complete idiot.'

She snorted, as if this was a matter of opinion. After a pause, she said, 'And when Gina was alive, did you ever masturbate about me?'

'Yes,' I said nervously. 'All the time.'

She withdrew her hand and released a long, laboured sigh.

I protested, 'Oh, come on, Natalie. You can't blame me for wanking.'

'I think I *can* blame you. In fact, I *do* blame you.'

'You were telling me you loved me five minutes ago.'

'That was before I knew you were a wanker.'

'Come off it. Have you never had a wank?'

Her nostrils flared. 'That's none of your business.'

I emitted a gay mocking laugh. Except it wasn't that gay. Or mocking. It wasn't much of a laugh, either.

She said, 'It isn't bloody well funny. You got the Ellen Quirke award! And all the time you were betraying women. You betrayed my sister twice. First by fucking me, and then by fucking Josephine.'

I said, 'I only fucked you in my imagination.'

'That makes no difference,' she retorted. 'Pornography begins at home.'

'What the bollocking hell is that supposed to mean?'

'For your information, it's Ellen Quirke's most famous statement. It's inscribed on the base of that award you're using as a fucking paperweight.'

Abruptly, she leapt to her feet. In a panic, I shouted, 'Natalie, you said you wouldn't hate me!'

She turned and looked down on me. She seemed to tower above me, like a female titan, seething with moral rectitude. 'No. I don't hate you. But I despair of you, Guy. I really do. You've let everyone down. Especially yourself.'

'Oh, please, Nat,' I pleaded. 'Sit down. Don't be like this.'

'The other day,' she intoned, 'when you were slagging off my friends . . . that was the real you talking, wasn't it? A world exclusive: Guy Lockheart as you've never seen him before. You must think women are pretty stupid.'

I stood to face her. 'No! No! I've never thought that.'

I grabbed her wrist. She wrenched it free. 'Don't touch me.'

I heard bleating in the distance.

'Now look what you've done,' I complained. 'You've woken up Erik.'

'Just fuck off,' she said.

'Natalie,' I whined. 'This isn't fair. It isn't fair to punish someone for being honest. Have you never read *Tess of the D'Urbervilles*?'

'Shut up,' she snapped. 'You're a fake, Guy.'

'Yes,' I acknowledged, trying to smile. 'But I'm *your* fake.' I reached for her again. Aggressively, she pushed me away.

'Don't fucking touch me!' she spat. 'Don't ever touch me again, you sexist bastard.'

Part Two

Sexists

The Sad Sexist

In the morning, I asked Natalie what she wanted to do. She said she didn't know, and needed time to think. I promised to stay with my brother until she reached some kind of decision. Ben and Rachel already lived in cramped conditions, but I knew it would be more comfortable to sleep on their lumpy sofa, and at least be treated with respect, than to sleep in my old bed at my parents' house and be subjected to prying questions and long murderous silences over breakfast.

Call me naïve, but I was astonished and bewildered by the prudish pomposity of Natalie's reaction. For her, my most shocking revelation had not been my adulterous fling with Jo, but the fact that I had treated her, the divine Natalie, as a sex object. Was this the same Natalie who had showered in front of me, and pretended not to notice my subsequent erection? Or invited me to father her child and witness its birth? Did she really imagine that I could behold a beautiful naked woman on a daily basis without wanting to invade her space? What kind of eunuch did she take me for?

Mingled with this sense of outrage, however, was the grim suspicion that I deserved everything I got. Or didn't get. A man who promotes himself as the first feminist saint can hardly complain if a woman who once admired his ideals is shocked by the smell of his balls. As Natalie had pointed out, I was a fake. For years, I had talked like Sidney de Beauvoir, and thought like Benny Hill.

But Benny Hill had feelings, and so did I, his true spiritual descendant. I became sick with love and hopeless yearning. I couldn't eat, and could scarcely say more than two words at a time to my brother or his wife. Young Sam, antagonized by my detached demeanour, took to hitting me over the head with an inflatable plastic hammer. I did nothing to defend myself, feeling that the young lout had a right to his opinion.

Ben tolerated my self-indulgent silence for two days, then took me aside to give me some advice. He put his arm around me and said, 'Cheer up, you daft twat.'

That was it. That was my brother's advice.

The call came, late at night, just as I was bedding down on the lumpy sofa. Natalie invited me over to her house, for cocoa and an ultimatum. My clapped-out Mini was still in the garage at Natalie's house, so I borrowed the bicycle that Rachel sometimes rode to the shops on. It had no lights, so I was forced to ride on the pavement. It was a lady's bike, too. I was riding a lady's bike, on the pavement, without lights, on the way to a house numbered thirteen, where the woman I loved was waiting to reveal my fate. Is this not a perfect (if rather overcrowded) metaphor for the predicament of the Western male in the closing stages of the twentieth century?

Natalie opened the door to me. She was dressed in black, from head to toe. I entered the house and, wordlessly, she led me upstairs. Hope stirred in my idiot bosom. Was this to be a grand reconciliation, complete with silk sheets, stockings and suspenders? But as we entered the room, where the only light came from the candles on the altar of Gina's shrine, I knew that a reconciliatory shag was not on the agenda.

Natalie stretched out a hand towards the bed, indicating that I should be seated. She herself remained standing, with her back to the flames. Eerie light, reflected from the blank walls, washed over her handsome face.

'I've decided what to do,' she disclosed.

'Yeah,' I anticipated. 'Fuck off, Guy. You're a sexist bastard. Fuck off and goodbye.'

With arresting serenity, she said, 'No, Guy. I can't just banish you from my life. Because, quite simply, you and Erik are the only family I've got.'

Touched by these kind words, I made to stand, but she repelled me by raising one finger. To me, the movement of that finger was as threatening as the sudden thrash of a cobra's coils.

'Don't touch me,' she warned. 'The non-touching rule still stands, and will remain in force until the time when you prove yourself worthy of physical affection. A time, of course, that may never come.'

'Fuck,' I gasped.

'And there *certainly* won't be any of that,' she stressed. 'You are not to touch me, kiss me, hold me or make any kind of advance towards me. Not until that time, that future time . . .'

'Which may never come,' I grumbled. 'Yeah. I get it. What's the fucking point, then? Eh? What's the point of loving someone you can't touch?'

'If you don't know, I can't tell you.'

I tutted in disgust. 'What is this, Natalie? The zen version of *University Challenge*?'

She shrugged, impervious to provocation. 'You've hurt a lot of women, Guy. I can't allow you back into my heart unless you're willing to fulfil certain conditions. Do you want to hear those conditions or not?'

I stared at her resentfully. I felt like walking out of that house, never to return. But I couldn't move. She was too beautiful. If you saw her, you'd understand.

I surrendered. 'Yeah. Sure. Tell me.'

147

'I'm going to set you a series of tasks,' she said. 'If you carry out these tasks to my satisfaction, I'll consider loving you.'

'As a brother?'

'No. As a lover.'

My face must have betrayed my pleasure, for she added, 'But when I say "tasks", I don't mean washing dishes, or taking out the rubbish. That'd be too easy. You were always willing to help with the housework.'

I nodded, glad to receive this crumb of praise. 'Yes, I've been a good little helper.'

'But housework is nothing,' she continued. 'I want you to do something rather more substantial for me. I want you to change lives, and, hopefully, change your own life in the process.'

'I refuse to work with old people,' I said.

'Did I say anything about old people?' she admonished. 'Stop interrupting.'

I apologized.

'Right, then. Your first task and your second task are to run concurrently. Your first task being, to write the truth about yourself for the editor of *Woman of Today*.'

'She'd never print it.'

'That doesn't matter. The truth is the truth, whether it's printed or not. Just show her what you're really like.'

'What do you expect me to do? Write a column about dancing around the house naked with your knickers on my head?'

'Why?' she asked quietly. 'Have you ever done that?'

'No,' I said.

'The truth, Guy,' she urged.

I gulped noisily. 'Yes,' I admitted.

She granted me a faint smile. 'Good,' she said. 'Then write about it. Chronicle all your lies and hypocrisy. Advertise your crimes. Let the women who've trusted you know what a slime-ball you've been.'

I puffed and pouted. 'Ariadne won't like it.'

'Good. Write about her, too. What do you think of her?'

'I think she's a silly horse-faced bitch. But she's got a good side.'

'You mean she gives you money?'

'Well, yes,' I conceded.

'Do you find her sexually attractive?'

'Er, hardly,' I replied. 'She's virtually unshaggable.'

Natalie nodded in approval. 'Good. Good. That's extremely offensive. You'd better write that down, as well.'

'I don't get this. Why do you want me to be sexist?'

'I don't *want* you to be sexist. You *are* sexist. I simply want you to be honest. Reveal yourself as you really are to those who've believed in you. Show women what bastards men can be. All the prejudice, the lust and contempt. No more pretence. Do you accept my challenge?'

'No. I mean, yes,' I said. 'Definitely yes.'

'The second task involves Josephine, who, I might add, has been phoning you daily.'

'Ah.'

'But you're not interested in her, are you?'

'No.'

'She's good enough to fuck, but not good enough to take to the pictures. Is that it?'

'It depends what the film is. Anything more intellectually taxing than *Snow White* would cause her serious problems.'

'You're not a nice person, Guy.'

'Fair comment,' I said.

'Josephine appears in pornographic magazines, doesn't she?'

'Well . . . no,' I said. 'Not real porn.'

149

'Really?' Natalie walked over to the bed, slipped her hand under the quilt and extracted a shiny new magazine. It was a copy of *Red Cheeks*.

'Now, that isn't mine!' I blurted defensively. 'I've never seen it before in my life.'

'I know,' said Natalie. 'I bought it myself. Come on, then. Show me. Which one of these poor, uneducated working-class women is Josephine?'

Self-consciously, I flicked through the magazine, finally pausing at a photo-spread in which two women dressed as cow-girls were whipping a cowboy in a barn. The cowboy was hanging by chains from the rafters, naked except for a white stetson and matching cowboy boots. 'It's hard to tell in this light,' I said morosely. 'But I think *this* is her.'

Natalie leaned over me. I inhaled her warm sweet fragrance. 'Which one?'

'This girl,' I said, tapping the guilty page. 'The one with the six-shooter up her arse.'

Natalie sighed, and walked over to the shrine. With her back to me, she said: 'And you say this isn't pornographic?'

'That's right,' I insisted. 'If it was real porn, that guy would have a ten-gallon prick to match his ten-gallon hat. The guy in the mag hasn't even got a hard-on, and his dick is only average.'

'It's as big as yours,' she said, turning to face me.

'Thanks,' I said. 'That's me. Mr Average.'

'Anyway, I think it's terrible that a woman you know, a woman that you've actually slept with, is forced to appear in dirty magazines.'

'She isn't forced,' I replied. 'Nobody's forcing her. It's just the only way she can make money.'

'Well, I think you should help her to find a better way. That's your second task. Teach her about feminism. Help her to find alternative employment.'

'Fuck!' I protested.

Natalie tilted her head to one side. 'That's the deal. Take it or leave it.'

'Oh, fucking, fucking hell!'

'Are you refusing to accept the second task?'

'No. No. I'll do it.'

'Good,' she said. 'In the meantime, while you're on trial, you may live here. In exchange, I expect you to baby-sit whenever necessary. But I'll allow you time off in order to fulfil the five tasks.'

'Five? I thought there were only two.'

'The remaining three tasks will be revealed to you when the first two are completed.'

'Shit, Natalie,' I moaned. 'This is ridiculous.'

With ponderous symbolism, she held the door open for me.

'I didn't mean it,' I said.

She closed the door and walked over to me.

'Sorry. But, Nat, changing a person's life is a pretty tall order. How will you know whether I've succeeded or not?'

'You'll find out,' Natalie assured me. 'It will all be revealed to you, at the appointed hour.'

The Sexy Sexist

I slept at Natalie's house that night, and in the morning rode back to Ben's on a lady's bike and picked up my things. In the afternoon, I sat down and wrote about myself for the readers of *Woman of Today*. Ariadne was still awaiting the first two chapters of *The Sympathetic Sexist*, but instead I decided to write about what had happened to me since I'd received the Ellen Quirke award.

It wasn't a novel. It was an autobiographical account, with the names, places and events unchanged. As soon as I stopped worrying about all that 'serious writer' shit, everything that I seriously believed about myself and those around me came pouring out. I wrote thirty pages in two days, the same pages that open this account. It wasn't particularly sympathetic, but it was the truth.

I showed the new material to Natalie, who read it while she was feeding the baby. When she'd finished, she nodded in approval and said 'Good. No one'll like you when they read this.'

'It'll mean the end of my career,' I said.

'Good. You'll have more time to concentrate on your other tasks.'

Josephine was waiting for me at Euston station. She was delighted to see me, believing that I'd arrived for a romantic weekend. When we'd arranged my visit over the phone, I'd avoided mentioning that I intended to introduce her to feminism and change her life. I didn't think she'd understand.

We took a taxi to Hammersmith, so that I could deposit my bags at her flat. She lived in Shepherd's Bush Road, where the heavy traffic roared and fumed. Her flat was situated above a TV repair shop. Her flat-mate, Mary, was a trainee beautician from Dublin. When we arrived, Mary was in the living room, being visited by about seven relatives, four of whom were small children. They were all laughing raucously and drinking tea. I couldn't hear what they were saying, but, no doubt, the conversation went something like this:

—Ah, now don't yer work too fucking hard, now, Mary.

—Jaysus, Conor, watch yer fucking language, yer dirty old shite, yen. And why is there fuckin' hyphens in front of every sentence we come out with?

—Fuck knows. It started with James Joyce, the old bollix. Then yer man, Roddy Doyle, he does it, too. Irish novelists have a morbid fear of the apostrophe, so they do . . .

In Josephine's room I placed my bag on the floor. 'Who the bloody hell are that lot?'

'They're all staying with us. They're Mary's family, they are. From Ireland.'

'Fucking Ada! I shouldn't imagine there's anyone left in Ireland, is there? They're all out there, drinking tea in your living room.'

Jo closed the door, came over to me and threw her arms around me. 'It don't matter, Guy. It's just us, in here.'

Gently, I extricated myself from her arms. 'Jo, before you start, I've got to tell you something.'

We sat on the bed, while I explained about Natalie. Jo's face grew sulky and resentful. I said that I loved Nat, and was fond of Jo, and felt she deserved better from life than having a Colt 45 shoved up her rectum. Jo, who felt that her work in *Red Cheeks* had been highly artistic, began to

153

get cross, until I mentioned Gina's death. Then I realized that Jo didn't know that my wife had died. Bomber hadn't told her, and neither had I. The news made her a little shaky.

'I s'pose you blame me, don't yer? I don't blame you if yer do, neither. I wouldn't really blame yer if you thought I was to blame for it being all my fault.'

'No,' I said firmly. 'I take full responsibility. But, that's why, really. That's why, from now on, things can't be the same between us.'

'Yeah,' she said, squeezing my leg. 'But we can still, you know, do it, kinda fing. Can't we?'

'No, Jo.'

'Aw.' She pressed her pornographic breasts against my arm. I could see her nipples poking through her T-shirt. 'Can't we?'

'No,' I said. 'Besides, Natalie would know.'

'She would never. Can't see us, can she?'

'Makes no difference, Jo. She'd still know, believe me. And even if she didn't know, I still love her.'

She started sulking. 'Fancy telling me that. You're saying she's better than me, you are.'

'No, I'm not.' I kissed her in a suitably brotherly fashion.

She began to pout like a small child. 'You've upset all me plans, now.'

'What plans?'

'We was goin' to go to bed and after, I was goin' to make yer cheese-on-toast and everyfink.'

'Never mind.'

'There was somethin' else, too. I 'ad a surprise for yer, an' now you've made me go and forget what it was.'

'It'll come to you. In the meantime, why don't we go out?'

'Where?'

'Anywhere.' An idea occurred to me. 'Kensington Gardens. Yeah. Let's go to Kensington Gardens.'

She looked puzzled. 'It's just a park, innit?'

'It's a nice park. Come on.'

'But ain't it just trees? I fawt it was just a load o' trees.'

(If Jo sounds like Eliza-fucking-Doolittle on a bad day, I'm sorry. But this was how she actually talked. I couldn't believe it, either.)

It was a hot afternoon, and the gardens were full of people, lying on the grass, playing ball-games, or just strolling hand in hand, like Josephine and me. She'd lived in London all her life, yet had never once visited Kensington Gardens, the Tower of London, Buckingham Palace or St Paul's Cathedral.

Josephine had never been anywhere.

I showed her the statue of Peter Pan. She regarded it dubiously, furrows appearing on her forehead. 'He looks like a bender. I never knew Peter Pan was meant to be a bender.'

'Barrie probably would have agreed with you,' I commented.

'Barry who?' said Jo.

As we walked, I tried to talk to her about the ethics of 'glamour photography'. Did she, for instance, realize that most men viewed her as a sex object?

'Oh, yeah,' she said. 'Men 'ave viewed me as a sex object all me life.'

I was encouraged. At least she seemed to know what a sex object was. 'And has it occurred to you that women aren't put on earth to be sex objects, but to be fully rounded human beings?'

'I'm fully rounded.' Jo smiled, nodding down at her voluptuous breasts. 'No complaints, there.'

'That isn't quite what I meant. I'm saying that you're not just a body, Jo. You've got a mind, too. But the men who wank over pictures of you – they're hardly thinking about your mind, are they?'

'Stop it.'

'Stop what?'

'You mustn't use words like that,' she said reprovingly.'

'What? Words like "mind"?'

'No. The other word.'

'Wank?'

She slapped my arm. 'Guy, stop it. I don't wancha talkin' that way.'

'But Bomber swears all the time.'

'That's cos 'e doesn't know any better. But you write for magazines an' that. You don't have ta use language.'

'That's true. OK. I'll put it another way: when you see photographs of yourself, how do you feel?'

'Depends. Depends how I look in the picture. You know what I mean? Whether they've made me look nice.'

'Oh. And how nice do you think you look with a revolver sticking out of your bum-hole?'

'Don't,' she said, more hurt than angry. 'Please, Guy. I don't like it when yer talk like that.'

'I'm sorry . . . I'm just trying to explain.'

'I'm a lady,' she said. 'An' I like to be treated like one.'

I sighed. We'd reached the Round Pond. The mid-afternoon sun was hot and bright. Tiny dazzling stars of fire were dancing on the surface of the water. A strong breeze came from nowhere, blowing Jo's long hair behind her so that she resembled the figurehead of a Norse ship.

I squeezed her hand affectionately. 'Did you know that Shelley used to sail toy boats across that pond? Isn't that amazing? Just think. Shelley might once have stood where we're standing now.'

'I don't know what yer talkin' about.'

'Shelley. The poet?'

'Never 'eard of 'im.' She gazed at me sadly. 'I 'spect you think I'm really thick, doncha?'

'No,' I insisted. 'No.'

'Yeah, yer do. You think I'm stupid. I don't blame yer. I *am* stupid.'

'There are different kinds of intelligence, Jo.'

'Yeah,' she said. 'An' I got the stupid kind.'

We ate at a crappy pizza restaurant, where you could consume as much decomposing salad as you liked for a fiver a head. It was a lousy meal, but the best I could afford. My Pathetic-Bastard-of-the-Year-Award money was running out fast, and the fee for my column was barely enough to keep Erik in nappies.

Jo didn't seem to mind, though. It was obvious that she was simply happy to be with me.

As I forked cold slimy pasta into my mouth, I said, 'What I've been trying to get at is: have you ever considered any other line of work? Apart from being a, well, er . . .'

'Model?' she offered.

'Yeah.' I almost choked on my own hypocrisy. 'That's the word.'

'Oh, yeah,' she said, trying to be sarcastic. 'I've considered loadsa fings. Yeah. I was even plannin' on goin' to university and gettin' a few A levels.'

'No, but really. Isn't there something else you could try?'

She looked doubtful. 'I tried being a waitress for a few nights. But I couldn't stick it.'

'Why?'

'You had to learn all the names of fings what were on the menu. It was all in French or summink. I mean, what's "pigon sauce", when it's at home?'

I confessed my bafflement, then realised that she meant *piquant* sauce.

157

'Then I tried bar work,' she said. 'And I got loads o' tips, an' all. Till I packed it in.'

'Why'd you pack it in?'

'Well, some of the customers asked for loads o' drinks, all at once, and not just the same drinks, neither. Know what I mean? I couldn't remember 'alf the things they asked me for.'

I sighed. 'But Jo, is there nothing you *want* to do? There must be something . . .'

Her face lit up. 'Yeah, yeah,' she enthused. 'Me big dream, me greatest ever ambition, since I was a little girl, was to be a big actress, an' be in films in 'ollywood.'

Trying to sound enthusiastic, I said, 'Yeah? Really?'

'Yeah. But, hey! You've reminded me. That was the surprise I wanted to tell yer about! I already *am* one. An actress, I mean. I done a video.'

A nasty feeling stole over me. 'You didn't make it with Bomber, by any chance?'

She laughed at the very idea. 'Nah! He couldn't act. But, listen, Guy, when we get back, I must show you me film. It was a proper speaking part, an' all. I got five hundred quid! Cash-in-hand. They used make-up and proper lights an' that. It was dead artistic.'

'And this video,' I enquired, already fearing the worst, 'would it have a title, by any chance?'

'Yeah,' said Jo, looking rather sheepish. 'It's called *Ram-Raid My Pussy.*'

That night, while Jo made coffee and jostled with friendly Irish brigands in the kitchen, I turned on her small colour portable, slotted the cassette of *Ram-Raid My Pussy* into a modest video-recorder, and lay on the bed to assess Josephine's grasp of dramatic technique.

In the first scene, Jo and a sexy young brunette were pictured in a living room. They were dressed in skimpy underwear, and the brunette, who had an American accent, was saying things like, 'Hey, you're really something. I'll bet you've got a real lush pussy.'

Jo's 'character' didn't say anything, just undressed when the brunette started to undress, then lay on the floor with her legs apart. Then, in the next shot, the brunette had buried her arm up to the wrist in Jo's inner sanctum. In no time at all, another woman, a hard-faced redhead, entered, stripped off and shoved her fist into the brunette. This carried on until there were six women in a circle, each being fisted and fisting some other poor cow in return. And there at the head of the tragic circle was sweet Jo herself, arm inside a dumpy middle-aged blonde who should have been serving school dinners.

I, myself, found the spectacle incredibly depressing, but my stupid bloody penis seemed to like it.

Jo came in with the coffee, glanced at the screen, and said: 'Don't watch that. Watch the bit where I do me acting.'

'Aren't you acting in this scene?' I asked, horrified, gesturing at the moaning, groaning heap of fallen women.

'Nah,' she said. She snatched the remote control from my grasp. 'You wanta be watching me speak.'

She fast-forwarded the film, which looked more or less the same all the way through, then let it play at a scene where Jo was alone in a room with a semi-naked West Indian. He had white paint on his face and he was wearing a grass skirt, out of which his erect dong was peeking.

'Ugga-mugga. White woman,' he said.

'Don't talk,' said the screen Jo, taking off her knickers. 'Just do it.'

Jo stopped the tape and beamed at me proudly. 'Well? Whatcha fink?'

'Was that your only line?'

'Yeah,' she said. 'Was I any good?'

'Yes.' I nodded. 'You were very convincing.'

159

She hugged herself with delight. 'Yeah. I was, wanni? They tried to make me say "Just do it, you black bastard." But I told 'em I wasn't gonna say anyfink like that, not if they paid me six hundred quid.'

'Because it wouldn't be lady-like?' I suggested.

'No,' she answered. ''Cause it ain't nice to black people.'

I slept on Jo's floor, or, rather, lay awake listening to the sound of the entire population of Ireland trooping backwards and forwards to the bathroom, all night long. More disturbing, however, was the knowledge that by my side lay a beautiful young woman who was willing to have sex with me. Yet I did not yield. I may have masturbated, but I did not yield.

My forbearance owed more to caution than honour. I felt that if I succumbed to temptation, Natalie would find out, not necessarily because she was psychic like Gina, but because poor daft Josephine would probably tell her.

In the morning, after breakfast, I gave Jo a crash course in sexual politics. I'd copied down some simple definitions from a dictionary, and was attempting to teach them to her. We sat on the bed, and went through the list together. But Jo had an alarmingly short attention-span.

'Once again, Jo: sexism. The belief that one gender is inherently inferior to another.'

'Whatcha goin' on about?'

'Sexism – you know, when men think that women don't have any, well, brains or spiritual value, or, for that matter, when women think the same about men. That's sexism.'

'So?'

'What do you mean "so"?'

'I can't find me other earring. Are yer sitting on it? Are yer?'

'Jo, will you stop fidgeting? I'm trying to talk to you.'

'Talk as much as yer like. Ain't gonna change nuffink.'

160

'No. Maybe not. That's a very valid point. But just for the sake of argument: if someone asked you for a definition of sexism, what would you say?'

'I'd say I need to go to the supermarket.'

'Eh?'

'I 'ave to go to the supermarket. We got no food in the 'ouse.'

'So that's your definition of sexism, is it? "Sexism is a state of having to go shopping when there's no food in the house."'

'Yeah.' She laughed throatily. 'If yer like.'

I gave her an audio-cassette on which I'd recorded a series of simple definitions. It was intended to be a kind of 'semi-literate guide to sexual politics'. I begged Jo to play the tape on her Walkman, and went home to Manchester.

It felt bad to leave her, but I didn't see what else I could do.

Back home in Hazel Grove, I told Natalie how I'd progressed. I couldn't just tell her downstairs, while she was doing the ironing. Oh no. She made me go up to my room, so that she could draw the curtains and light the candles in front of Gina's shrine. Then she placed her mother's old wicker chair before the shrine and seated herself, looking more like a High Priestess than ever.

'All right,' she announced. 'Now you can speak.'

I described my sojourn with Jo, leaving nothing out. 'And the truth is, I can't think of a job she could do. Not one that'd make her happy. She says she wants to be an actress, but I can't see it, myself. And as for making her understand about sexual politics, honestly, Natalie, I'd stand more chance of fucking the PM up the arse during Question Time in the House of Commons.'

Expressionlessly, Natalie said, 'All right.'

'What? You want me to fuck the prime minister?'

161

'No. I mean you shouldn't do anything you don't want to do.'

Sweet relief blossomed inside me. 'Yeah,' I said. 'I tried, didn't I? At least I tried.'

'Yes, Guy. You tried and failed. You've got a week to pack up your things and move out.'

'Why?' I suddenly sounded like a castrato. 'Why should I?'

'I set you a task, Guy. And what happens? You give up after four days. It's not exactly an impressive record, is it?'

'But, Natalie, be fair. What you've asked me to do is fucking-twatting-and-prostitutingly-well impossible.'

'No. I don't agree. Difficult, yes. But not impossible.'

I sighed. I was lost for words, frankly.

Natalie observed me tolerantly. 'It's not easy to help other people, is it, Guy? It's not always easy to love them, either. But if you can't do better than this, you'll never win my heart.'

I went to visit Charles. As far as I could see, he was my only hope. He lived on the upper floor of a large rambling house in Sale, Cheshire, and his quarrelsome father occupied the ground floor. Father and son, having stopped pretending to have a normal relationship years ago, now used separate entrances, and led separate lives.

It was a peculiar arrangement. Charles was allowed to live there, rent-free, because his father couldn't bear the thought of living alone, and Charles couldn't bear the thought of paying rent. Yet each man hated the sight of the other, and only communicated by a system of raps and bangs, and, in emergencies, the odd terse sentence. It was difficult to decide whether their mutually agreed estrangement showed extraordinary stupidity or refreshing maturity.

Charles lived in a state of elegant disarray. Everything on

162

his floor was expensive, but in the wrong place, or in the right place, but covered in dust. Tonight, he seemed edgy and slightly unsure of himself. This was something I'd noted before, whenever it had been his turn to entertain the men's group. Most of the time, he was our resident court jester: the man least likely to blow his nose in a crisis. But here, on his own ground, he seemed less able to pretend that life was a joke – perhaps because he was surrounded by the trappings and the debris of his all-too-solitary, all-too-unfunny life.

None the less, he served me coffee, and moved a pile of brand-new paperbacks on to the floor for me, enabling me to sit down. I placed the orange A4 folder that I'd brought with me on top of the books while I drank my coffee. From time to time I saw Charles eyeing the folder warily, possibly surmising that it contained his destiny.

'Cut to the chase, old sport,' said Charles. 'What can I do for you?'

I told him about Natalie's reaction to my declaration of love, and her demand that I fulfil a series of tasks, commencing with the rehabilitation of Josephine.

'Dear me,' he reflected darkly. 'The woman's a fucking crack-pot.'

'I know,' I said. 'But I still love her.'

'No, no, no. It's not on. You can't saddle yourself with a loony, my dear chap. She'll be asking you to perform tricks for the rest of your life. On your wedding night, it'll be, "Convert the Pope to Buddhism, then I'll let you see my twat. But only from a distance." Who does she think she is? A princess in a story by the decidedly Grimm brothers? No, Guy. I'm sorry, but it's no good. You'll have to tell her to shove her holy quests up her royal botty-hole.'

'I can't, Charles. I'm in love with her. Besides, there's Erik to consider.'

He gazed at me wistfully. 'Well, I've given you my advice, chum. The rest is up to you, as an astonishingly unhelpful bastard would say.'

'I came to ask for help, Charles. Not advice.'

'Oh?' He immediately looked suspicious. 'I'm not that well off for cash myself, if that's what you mean.'

'No. I'm not after a loan. It's about Josephine ... she wants to be an actress, and, well, you're a director.'

He sighed impatiently.

'Let me finish,' I said. 'If she had one line, or even a walk-on in something, it'd be a way of showing Natalie that I've tried ... and it'd be a damn sight better for Jo than appearing in *Shaft Me Senseless*.'

'What you perhaps don't appreciate, Guy,' Charles answered suavely, 'is that television doesn't quite work like that. We employ casting directors for that sort of thing. Not really my department, you understand.'

Without comment, I reached into the orange folder, and produced Natalie's copy of *Red Cheeks*. Opening the magazine on the appropriate page, I passed it over to Charles. He placed his coffee cup on the floor, his heavy jaw sagging as he blinked and marvelled at the images before him.

'She's the girl in the black hat,' I said, helpfully.

'Good Lord above!' he exclaimed. 'But the lady's got a marvellous chest. Like one of the fucking Rhine Maidens. Simply astounding!'

'She's certainly well made.'

'And you're telling me that you enjoyed repeated acts of joyous copulation with a woman like that?'

'No. Not a woman *like* that. With *that* woman. But listen, Charles. I don't want her just to show her tits. I want her to have a couple of lines of dialogue. You know? A small character part. Otherwise, Natalie will just say I'm moving Jo from one porn film to another.'

His demeanour had altered radically. He now appeared

eager to accommodate me. 'But of course. Message understood. In any case, Granada TV don't go in for tits, or explicit filth generally. Worse fucking luck. I'd love to see wide-open beaver shots of some of the women from *Coronation Street*. Wouldn't you? But anyway, leave me the lady's details, old son, and I'll do my fucking best.'

We chatted idly for a while longer. Then I scribbled down Jo's address and phone number on a scrap of paper and passed it to Charles. As I got up to leave, I attempted to return *Red Cheeks* to its folder, but Charles tugged the magazine out of my fingers.

'Er, I think I'd better hang on to that, Guy. If you don't mind? Purely for research purposes, you understand?'

I understood.

The morning after, while Nat was in the garden playing with Erik, and I was cleaning the lavatory, the phone rang. I rushed downstairs to answer it, expecting to hear from Charles. Instead, a middle-aged, middle-class woman said, 'Guy? Guy Lockheart?'

'Yes?' I said, not recognising the voice.

'It's Ariadne.'

'Oh.' I braced myself.

She sounded ineffably weary. 'What *are* you doing? I mean, what do you *imagine* you're achieving?'

'Ah,' I remarked. 'You've read my stuff, I take it?'

'Stuff and bloody nonsense, I call it,' she replied, demonstrating all the wit of a menopausal traffic warden. 'What have I ever done to you? Eh? What have I done, that you should describe me as, where is it?' (A rattle of pages.) 'Here we are: "a strident horse . . . face covered in ochre-coloured mud . . . has never had a decent orgasm in her life". Why, Guy? *Why?*'

'I've insulted other people, too. I actually think you got off rather lightly.'

165

'Oh, *do* you? But I notice that you've been surprisingly easy on yourself.'

'No. I'm as shitty as everyone else. But at least I *know* I'm shitty. Or, to put it another way, "In the country of the turd, the man with toilet paper is king."'

'What *are* you talking about? You're babbling, do you realize that? Are you on drugs or something?'

'No. But talking of drugs, how's your hormone replacement therapy going? Any hope of you becoming a woman again, or what?'

A long, considered sigh. 'I think we ought to have this conversation another time, when you're feeling more yourself.'

'I *am* myself!' I cried in exasperation. 'This is the real me. I'm a horrible, cynical bastard.'

'No, Guy. I know what horrors you've been through lately, and you're trying to take your anger out on other people. You can't fool me, doll. This is Ariadne you're talking to.'

There is nothing more infuriating than trying to burn one's boats, and then hearing the merry tring-tring of approaching fire engines. 'Oh, come on, Ariadne. Sack me. I'm a liar and a fraud.'

'Sack you? Why would I want to do that, for God's sake?'

'I'm crap! I'm a liar and a sexist creep.'

'Even if that were true, which it patently is not, you also happen to be my best writer.'

'You can't just leave it at that. I'm a charlatan, Ariadne. I've lied to you and your sub-human readers.'

'I'm sure we'll recover. Don't take it all so seriously, darling. It's only a magazine, designed to sell advertising space. Relax, Guy. You're mine for keeps. Ring me in a few days, when you've calmed down.'

Quietly, Ariadne put the phone down, leaving me flattened and amazed. I'd been anticipating a fierce confrontation, a seething exchange of bilious acrimony. In case things got nasty, I'd prepared two vicious one-liners:

1) You're just a sad old bag with a cunt like a sun-dried tomato.

2) Every time you cross your legs, your labia creak like rusty door hinges.

Now, because of my editor's confounded generosity, both of these insults would be wasted. Nor could I use them on my mother, who had never heard of labia *or* sun-dried tomatoes.

After nine days Jo phoned to tell me, excitedly, that she'd met Charles and been offered a small part in a new Granada drama serial. Delighted and amazed, I literally whooped for joy.

'It's not a specially big part,' she explained. 'But Charles says it's crucial to the dramatic whatsername.'

'Development?'

'No. Summink that begins with "n".'

'Dénouement?'

'Yeah, yeah. The newment.'

'But what does your character have to do, exactly?'

'Er, dunno, really.'

'Jo, he's not asking you to take your clothes off, is he?'

'I told yer, I dunno. The script's too fick. I 'aven't bin able to find me part, yet.'

Concerned, I spent money I could ill afford on a saver return to London, and met Jo at Euston station. She looked positively radiant, ablaze with her latest triumph. She'd brought the script along, and we searched through it together at the station buffet, over two plates of runny eggs, luke-warm beans and squashed, given-up-for-dead chips.

167

The drama concerned the misadventures of a promiscuous female MP. It was called *The Sexual Politician*, and was written by someone with the tantalizingly familiar name of Dudley Fingerman.

'What's your character called?' I asked her.

'Sindy,' she said proudly. 'Like the doll.'

After a struggle, I located Josephine's role. It occupied one third of a page, in a script that was two hundred pages long. Sindy, unsurprisingly, turned out to be a 'vice-girl'. She appeared in a scene at the Sexual Politician's country house, a birthday present from the heroine to her husband, Randolph.

Jo had one line of dialogue.

INT. NIGHT. RANDOLPH'S BEDROOM.
Enter RANDOLPH, *alone and drunk. He begins to undress. Then in mirror, he sees* SINDY *lying on the bed. She is as naked as we can get away with.*

> RANDOLPH: Great Scott! Where on earth did you spring from?
>
> SINDY (*Licks her lips*): Don't talk. Just do it.

The Seven Sexists

Natalie granted me another audience in front of the shrine. This time, the stately mystique of the occasion was marred somewhat by the sound of Erik, crying like a baby. Natalie held the small pink one over her shoulder, patting and soothing him every time he launched into a fresh fit of histrionics.

'So that's the story so far,' I said, summing up. 'Ariadne thinks I've been driven crazy by grief. And Josephine's going to be on the telly.'

I had omitted to mention that the gentle cockney's acting début required her to be 'as naked as we could get away with'. After all, there was always a chance that the programme would never be made, or that Natalie would renounce all her feminist ideals before it was screened. Just as there was always a chance that my penis would triple in size by Christmas.

I mean, you never know.

Natalie nodded appreciatively. 'You've done well.'

'Have I?'

'Yes. I'm impressed. You revealed your true self to your editor. It's not your fault if she can't accept the truth. And as for Josephine, well, I think that both you and she should be extremely proud of yourselves. How are her women's studies coming along?'

'Oh, they're coming. Along, that is.'

'Good. I'll look forward to discussing the issues with her when we meet.'

I almost fell off the bed. 'What? Why? When are you meeting her?'

'I've told you. At the appointed time.'

'When, though? When is it?'

'It'll be revealed to you, when the third and fourth tasks are completed.'

Erik filled his nappy loudly. I took this as a sign that he was on my side.

'OK,' I sighed. 'Are you going to tell me what these fucking tasks are?'

'Yes,' said Natalie. 'The third and fourth tasks shall run concurrently. The third task being, to make your brother renounce violence. The fourth task being, to convert your friend Bomber to feminism, and to make him cry. I want him to get in touch with his emotions.'

'Not asking for much, are you?' I grumbled sarcastically.

The smell of Erik's latest outrage was beginning to fill the room. I got up to leave.

'Wait,' said Natalie. 'I haven't told you about the fifth task.'

'I'm not sure I want to hear it,' I said.

'If you carry out the third and fourth tasks successfully, the fifth should more or less fulfil itself.'

I didn't like the sound of this at all.

'Go on,' I prompted.

'The fifth task is as follows: when I see Ben and Bomber together at the appointed time, I want them to be holding hands.'

'Oh, she's taking the piss,' scoffed Gordon.

The other members of my men's group agreed. That included Vaughan, who always considered both sides of an argument, even when there was only one side, or there was no argument to consider.

'I have to go with the general flow of popular opinion,'

Vaughan informed me. He tutted like an elderly maiden aunt. 'I think this Natalie woman is making an utter fool of you, and you're so desperate to win her favour that you just can't see it.'

'I told him the same thing, weeks ago,' said Charles grimly. Catching my eye, he added, 'I did, didn't I? I told you. She's taking you for a cunt.'

I was angry with them all. 'Shut up, Charles. You're the cunt.'

'No, you're the cunt,' he affirmed without malice.

'No, *you* are,' I countered cleverly. 'What's more, you're a smug cunt.'

'Better than being a stupid cunt.'

'Well, I think the pair of you are stupid cunts,' said Gordon.

'Well, that makes you an interfering cunt,' I told Gordon.

'I quite agree,' said Charles. He glanced down at Gordon's protuberant midriff. 'Not to mention a fat cunt.'

Malcolm was so incensed by this exchange that he pounded the ground with both fists. 'Stop it! Stop it! Stop it!'

It was a hot, cloudless Saturday afternoon in July. I'd called an emergency meeting, in view of my ridiculous predicament. We were all sitting on the lawn in the back garden of Vaughan's house, in the village of Poynton. Despite the pleasant weather, Vaughan's wife and children had been asked not to stray into the garden, lest they interrupt the profound thought-processes of five grown men who were calling each other cunts.

Vaughan, feeling that an interlude was in order, bellowed in the direction of the house. 'Fliss! Fliss? Any sign of that lemonade?'

Fliss was Vaughan's wife. Her real name was Felicity. She was a bony malcontent with translucent skin and masses of wiry ginger hair. I don't think she approved of Vaughan, or

171

his men's group. Because of her huge front teeth, I privately thought of her as 'Dental Fliss'. Privately, because it was such a feeble pun.

Fliss thrust her red-head through the open french window. 'What?' she demanded harshly.

Miming dehydration, Vaughan pointed to his throat and allowed his tongue to hang out, reminding me for all the world of Oliver Hardy. 'Lemonade, love. We're parched.'

She scowled and disappeared into the house.

'Actually, I've changed my mind.' Charles smiled.

'About what?' said Gordon and I simultaneously.

'Guy isn't a cunt. I'm the cunt. I'm a big, posh, silly cunt,' Charles proclaimed.

Malcolm wriggled in irritation. '*Please*. Will you stop *using* that word? It's so horribly misogynistic.'

'You were saying, Charles?' coaxed Vaughan.

'Merely that I regret my use of the four-letter word CUNT! The CUNT word. A vulgar term meaning a lady's CUNT.'

'Any more of this, and I'm leaving,' threatened Malcolm. 'This group is losing all sense of direction.'

Vaughan said, 'We're sorry you feel that way, Mal.'

'It gets more like a rugby-club outing every time we meet,' continued Malcolm, his spectacles glinting with emotion. How can spectacles express emotion? I don't know, but Malcolm's did. 'Why do we always have to plumb the depths? Why aren't we addressing the post-feminist debate?'

'Where is it?' joked Charles. 'Tell me where it is, and I'll address it and post it right back to you.'

'We were discussing Guy's problems,' pointed out Gordon, fanning himself with a white baseball cap. 'Don't you find his problems interesting?'

Malcolm nodded. 'Yes. Very. I just don't find misogyny very interesting. Or edifying.'

After a pause, I said, 'Anyway, that's the story so far. Nat

172

wants me to work miracles with Ben and Bomber. That's all she's asking for: miracles. Any ideas?'

No one said a thing. The sound of church bells whirled over the sweet summer lawns towards us. Some poor sods were getting married. In a neighbouring garden children laughed and splashed in a paddling pool.

'Fliss? Fliss, love?' shouted Vaughan. 'You've not forgotten, have you?'

'No suggestions, then?' I said. 'I'm on my own, am I? Thanks a lot. It's all your fault that I'm in this situation.'

'Why's it our fault?' asked Gordon with surprise.

'Because you advised me to tell Natalie the truth. All of you. You fucking did. I might be happy, now, if it weren't for you lot.'

Vaughan hummed philosophically. 'Emotions *are* rising high today. Must be the heat.'

Gordon said, 'I've got a suggestion.'

'What?' I asked him.

'Why don't we take your brother and this other guy to Devon with us at the end of the month?'

'Hey, now. There's a thought . . .' mused Vaughan.

'There'd be no room for them, would there?' I objected.

'Should be,' said Vaughan. 'The house is meant to sleep eight.'

'The only trouble is,' I said, 'is that I'd never get 'em there. Ben hates Bomber. He'd never agree to spend a weekend under the same roof.'

'Lie to him,' proposed Gordon.

'Yes,' said Charles. 'Invite your brother without mentioning this Bomber character. It'd be a nice surprise for him.'

'I don't agree,' sulked Malcolm. 'That's a terrible idea.'

We asked him why.

'By bringing in outsiders, we risk upsetting the delicate infrastructure of the group. What about the "strict confidentiality" ruling? How can we expect men who are mere visitors to the group to respect the need for secrecy? Or to even understand it?'

'But, Malcolm,' said Vaughan. 'In all the time I've known you, you haven't told me anything that I couldn't tell anyone outside the group.'

Malcolm raised his finger in accusation. 'I hope that doesn't mean you've betrayed a confidence, Vaughan?'

'No. Of course it doesn't! I'm just saying, well, I'm just saying . . . oh, God knows what I'm saying.'

Charles said, 'He's just saying that he hasn't told anyone about you, because there's nothing to tell. I mean, who the fuck'd be interested?'

'Yes, thank you, Charles,' said Malcolm. 'Thank you very much.'

'Anyway,' intervened Gordon, diplomatically. 'We'll just need to be discreet for a couple of days. Keep our most intimate problems to ourselves. Shouldn't be too difficult, surely? We'll be mainly working with Guy. And his brother and this "Bummer" fella.'

'Er, that's "Bomber",' I said.

'Come on, Mal,' urged Vaughan. 'Can't you go along with it, for Guy's sake? Plus, the more people sharing the house, the cheaper it works out.'

'Ah. But, unless I'm woefully mistaken, cheapness wasn't the purpose of the weekend,' Malcolm averred. 'I was under the impression that we were pilgrims seeking spiritual catharsis, not louts in search of a bargain-break in Blackpool. And from a personal point of view, the value that I place on this group is beyond rubies.'

He paused, waiting for Charles to say 'Beyond Ruby's what?' But the expected jest failed to manifest itself. After taking a deep breath, Malcolm resumed, 'This group has given me a great deal of support, while I've been splitting up from my partner.'

'And the break-up's been long and painful for you,' Gordon reminded him.

'Yes, thank you, Gordon. That's a good point,' nodded Malcolm, unaware that he was being teased. 'And over the past two years, I've learned to trust you all. The intervention of strangers could, I feel, ruin everything.'

A wasp buzzed close to his face, and he rolled over and kicked the air until it caught a whiff of him and dived for cover.

When he'd composed himself, I said, 'Malcolm, I hear what you say. But could we try it? Just for my sake?'

Malcolm regarded me dolefully. I gave him a winning smile. 'All right,' he said. 'For Guy's sake. As long as you all recognize that I'm not happy.'

The group passed a motion, officially recording our recognition of Malcolm's not-happiness. Then Vaughan's wife emerged from the house, carrying a tin tray. On the tray were glasses, a biscuit barrel and a large jug of iced home-made lemonade.

Vaughan clapped his hands together gleefully. 'Ahh!' he beamed. 'About time.'

The rest of us winced, feeling that Vaughan's words could have been more carefully chosen. Sure enough, Fliss yanked the jug off the tray and tipped its entire contents over Vaughan's head.

'Yes!' she ranted. 'About time! About bloody time you grew up! And the same goes for the rest of you!' With this, she hurled down the tray and flounced back into the house. The biscuit barrel hit Gordon on the head.

'Shit!' he complained to Vaughan, rubbing his bruised cranium. 'Can't you keep your wife in order?'

Vaughan just sat there, with crushed ice and lemonade dripping off his chin. 'Oh, judge for yourself. What does it bloody well look like?' he said forlornly.

*

I phoned Bomber, who was delighted to be invited to Devon. 'It'll be sound as a pound. The wife's off to a Fitness Instructors convention that weekend. I can dump the kids with the parents and fuck off to the seaside with you, you queer bastard.'

Ben was less enthusiastic. What horrified him most was the thought of spending a weekend with a 'bunch of perves'. He'd reached the conclusion that the members of my men's group were perverted after hearing that we sometimes held hands. But when I explained that I wanted to be closer to him, and to break down any barriers that had been erected between us by time, our parents, and our own ignorant fears, he seemed to understand.

'OK. This is the deal: I'll go, as a favour to you, and for no other reason. But if anyone tries to fondle me bollocks, I'll be off like a shot,' he stressed.

'Fair enough, Ben.'

We set off at noon on the last Friday in July, and motored south in Ben's gaudy Merc. The house Vaughan had rented overlooked a sheltered cove along the coast from Coombe Martin in north Devon. It was large, dilapidated and slightly damp, with a sloping, overgrown garden. A gate in the fence led to a narrow path, our only route down to the stony beach below.

When we arrived, Malcolm, Charles and Vaughan were in the garden, cooking sausages and burgers on a barbecue. At the sight of them, Ben assumed his least friendly expression, the one he normally reserved for Tory Party canvassers and Jehovah's Witnesses.

Greetings were exchanged. Ben nodded and grunted. 'Anyone else here?' I enquired nervously, glancing up at the house.

Vaughan lowered his toasting fork to say, 'Gordon's let us down.'

'You're joking.'

'Lamentably not,' confirmed Charles. 'I was supposed to be giving him a lift, but his wife rang to announce that he had an ingrown toe-nail.'

'What a pile of shit,' I remarked.

'Yes,' said Vaughan, with displeasure. 'You can always rely on Gordon to let you down. We've all known that for a long time, but if he thinks he's going to get away without paying his share of the rent, he's got another think coming.'

Ben had slouched over to the fence, and was staring moodily down at the sea, as if he was about to accuse it of looking at him. While he was out of earshot I said, 'No sign of Bomber?'

They shook their heads.

Hopefully, I said 'Maybe he won't turn up.'

The house had four bedrooms. Vaughan and Charles were sharing a room, and so were Ben and I. Malcolm had been allowed a room of his own, for obvious olfactory reasons. Bomber, if and when he turned up, would occupy the room at the front of the house, without a sea view. That was to be his reward for being the last to arrive.

When Ben saw the double bed in our bedroom, he started snarling. 'Jesus, I've never slept with a fucking bloke in my life, and I'm not about to start now.'

'But I'm your brother.'

He clearly wanted to deny this, but knew that medical evidence was on my side. 'Just don't try to bum me, that's all.' Angrily, he threw his luggage down on to the bed. 'And don't fart either.'

We sat around in the garden, eating burnt sausages and drinking bottled beer that Vaughan had had the foresight to chill. The open air and the congenial company did nothing to improve Ben's spirits. When Charles mentioned that he'd started hunting out locations for his new TV series, Ben dismissed all television as 'shit'.

'Yes, I know,' said Charles amiably. 'Especially the pro-grammes I make. Why? What do you do?'

'Fuck all,' mumbled Ben.

'Yes, he does. Tell 'em what you do for a living, Ben.'

'No. They'd only be fucking bored.'

Gamely, Malcolm denied this. 'Well, I, for one, would very much like to hear about Ben's job.'

'So would I,' chipped in Vaughan charitably.

With reluctance, Ben started to explain about ink sprock-ets and computerized press gauges, and I saw everyone's eyes slowly glaze over with boredom. Ben saw this too, and said bitterly, 'See? No one knows what I do for a living because no one can be bothered listening till I've finished fucking well telling 'em.'

Events took a turn for the worse when the gate leading to the front of the house creaked open and Bomber burst through. He was wearing candy-striped shorts and an undersized T-shirt that exposed his pale blubbery stomach.

'Greetings, shit-bags!' he cheerfully proclaimed.

Ben released an impassioned groan. 'Christ! That's all we fucking need!'

Unsettled by the manner of his reception, Bomber hovered uncertainly on the edge of the lawn, until Charles walked over and offered to show him to his room. The two men disappeared into the house.

Ben started cursing and pacing up and down. 'You lying bastard!' he said to me. 'You fucking knew, didn't you? You *knew* that tosser was coming . . .'

Malcolm and Vaughan lowered their eyes and stared at the grass, pretending to be impartial in that way that cowardly bastards have.

'Ben. Why don't you calm down?'

But he turned his back on me and stormed into the house.

Anxiously, Malcolm and Vaughan got to their feet.

Malcolm said, 'I do hope there won't be any violence.'

'So do I,' I said grimly.

'Yes,' said Vaughan. 'I take it your brother has been notified of the group's "no hitting" rule?'

'It wouldn't make any difference if he had,' I replied.

They followed me through the french windows into the dusty living room. We found Charles and Bomber in the kitchen. Charles was brewing a pot of tea, while Bomber sat at a rickety kitchen table, rolling a spliff.

He glanced up at me incuriously. 'Whadya want, ugly?'

'Where's Ben?'

'He just took off in his car,' answered Bomber.

'That's right,' verified Charles. 'Where's he going?'

'Fuck knows,' I sighed.

'Hey!' jested Bomber. 'Who're you calling "Fuck-nose"?'

'It isn't funny,' I said. 'Ben's buggered off, because of you.'

Bomber shrugged. He was liberally sprinkling dope along a line of tobacco. 'Nothing to do with me, pal.'

Malcolm was standing beside him. Bomber suddenly sniffed the air and grimaced. 'Whew! Has someone shat their pants, or what?'

Ben's disappearance had depressed me. The evening got worse before it got better. It had been Vaughan's idea to postpone group work until the morrow, and spend our first night by bonding in a convivial atmosphere. With this aim in mind, we retired to the living room. Hoping for a party, Bomber had brought along a crate of strong German beer and a couple of hard-core porn videos. 'Women and dogs, women and donkeys, even donkeys and dogs. Should be a real fucking laugh.'

Then he discovered that there was no TV or video. 'Bollocks!' he complained, crestfallen. 'Don't tell me I've got to look at you lot all night.'

179

'We could always act out the videos,' I suggested. 'I'll play the dog. You can be the donkey.'

Nobody laughed.

Even Charles seemed unusually subdued. 'You seem unusually subdued, Charles,' I said.

He smiled enigmatically. 'If you want the truth, I'm in love.'

'Who with?'

'You know that little totty you introduced me to?'

'Who? Josephine?'

He nodded proudly. 'I've been fucking her.'

Forgetting that Bomber had not been apprised of the recent developments in Jo's life, I said, 'What? You've really been fucking Jo?'

Charles smirked. 'She wanted to be an actress, and now she performs three times a night. It's made a new man of me. Or, to misquote Blake, "What a bosom, what an arse, to twist the sinews of my heart."'

His feminist principles submerged under several fathoms of alcohol, Vaughan said, 'What? You mean you've actually been having sex? Actually inserting your penis into her vagina, as it were? And keeping going until one or both of you attain orgasm?'

Malcolm never drank, and was therefore his sober, non-sexist self. The topic under discussion had turned his mouth into a thin jagged line, like the crack in an eggshell. It looked like the mouth of Dennis the Menace from *The Beano*, when Dennis is about to be slippered by his dad.

Ingenuously, Bomber turned to me and winked. 'You and me know a Josephine, too, don't we, mate?'

After my initial indiscretion, I was praying that the others would have the brains to keep quiet. Unfortunately, Vaughan said, 'It's the same girl, isn't it? I thought it was the same girl . . .'

Bomber's mouth dropped open. 'It's not, is it?'

180

With genteel regret, Charles said, 'I rather think it is, old chap.'

'Bloody hell!' gasped Bomber. 'You mean you've been fucking my bird?'

Charles smiled apologetically.

Bomber turned to me. 'I don't believe it. He sits there, bold as a cunt, and informs me he's having sexual intercourse.'

I said, 'We thought you'd finished with her.'

'Have I fuck finished with her!' exploded Bomber. 'Still got a fanny, hasn't she?'

'But you didn't mind when *I* fucked her,' I pointed out.

'That's different,' insisted Bomber bitterly. 'You were invited!'

'Sorry,' said Charles. 'But I didn't seek her out, if it's any help. Guy introduced us.'

'Thanks, Charles,' I said. 'Thanks a lot.'

'I can't believe it,' repeated Bomber, staring into my eyes. 'There he is smiling, drinking my fucking beer, and he has the bare-faced fucking cheek to say he's poking my girl-friend.' He turned his attention back to Charles. 'I suppose you've been shagging my wife, too?'

Charles shrugged. 'Let's face it: someone has to.'

Bomber spluttered with indignation, then without warning, burst out laughing. 'You cheeky bastard!'

From that moment forth, Bomber and Charles were officially in love.

Ben returned late that night. I was glad to see him, but tried not to show it. He staggered into our room while I was lying in bed, leafing through Sammy Kumquat's acclaimed book about bereavement: *I'm Not Dead If You're Not Dead*. Vaughan had loaned me the book, hoping that it would help me to come to terms with Gina's death.

'What're you reading?' demanded Ben. He was drunk.

I showed him the cover. He squinted at the book's title. Then, without ceremony, he snatched Kumquat's masterpiece out of my hand and hurled it through the open window.

'Ben!' I complained. 'That isn't my book.'

Struggling to remove his shoes, he said, 'Can't have you reading crap like that. You'll end up as queer as the rest of 'em.'

'The rest of who?'

'The fellas you're in this fucking . . . fucking thingy with.' He couldn't bring himself to say 'group': the word was far too effeminate for him.

Sitting on the bed, he leaned forward to confide in me. 'Haven't you fucking noticed? They're all gay.'

'Balls, Ben.'

'I'm not kidding,' he stressed. 'They're practically hairdressers!'

'Absolute crap.'

'Don't tell me you can't see it. Especially the big snobby one, and that little bastard who smells. Didn't you see the way they were looking at us? I'm telling you, mate. They fancy each other, they definitely fancy you, and I've got a nasty fucking feeling they fancy me, too . . .'

I was about to accuse him of homophobia when he stumbled off to brush his teeth. A few minutes later, I was jerked out of a doze by a sudden sharp pressure in my rear end. I turned round and saw Ben grinning and holding a toothbrush.

He leered unpleasantly. 'That's for inviting Lancaster without telling me.'

'Aw, no,' I groaned, rubbing my arse. 'Not the toothbrush.'

'Yes,' he said. 'And what's worse, it's your *own* toothbrush.'

When I was twelve and Ben had been fourteen, he used to

wait until I was asleep before jabbing me sharply up the rectum with the handle of his toothbrush. It had been a regular habit of his – just a friendly way of saying, 'You're a little bastard and I hate you.'

Now, laughing, he stripped down to his underpants and climbed into bed. 'Oh, I've missed that old toothbrush trick.'

I switched off the bedside lamp. 'You can be a right twat at times,' I said.

We lay awake in the dark for a while, listening to the rhythmic sighing of the sea. 'I think I might go home tomorrow,' he said.

'Naw, don't. Why?' I entreated. 'I need you here.'

I explained about Natalie, and the tasks she'd set me, missing out the one about Ben holding hands with Bomber. I didn't think he was ready for that.

After listening in silence, he said, 'Don't you think that girl's a bit fucking puddled? *I* think she is. She's bent, Guy. You'd be better off without her.'

'I love her, though. I've loved her for years.'

He sighed. 'I don't know. You had a lovely-looking wife, brainy, nice personality, and you weren't fucking satisfied.'

'No,' I said. 'But I did love her.'

There was a pause.

'So did I,' he said.

'As a friend, you mean?'

'No,' he replied. 'As a lovely fucking bird, the kind that you dream about.'

After a silence I said, 'But you've got Rachel.'

'Yeah. I know.'

'Rachel's gorgeous. And a nice person.'

'I know. I'm daft. But there you go. I always thought Gina was a bit of class. Too good for you, anyway. I used to fancy her something rotten.'

Not thinking, I said, 'Did you ever do anything about it?'

183

'Only once or twice . . .'

'*What?*'

I heard him sniggering. 'I'm joking, you dickhead.'

'Ah. About fancying Gina?'

'No. That part's true.'

'Ben, this is important. Why don't you tell the group about this tomorrow?'

'Fuck off! It's none of their business.'

'But that's what we're here for: to be honest.'

He yawned. 'I don't mind being honest with you, but not with a bunch of gay homosexuals.'

'OK,' I said, slightly dazed by his revelation about Gina. 'Night, then.'

He farted loudly and fell asleep.

In the morning, while Ben was sitting in the garden, eating his toast alone, Bomber walked out and handed him a cylindrical object wrapped in brown paper. I saw this through the kitchen window, and went to see what was happening.

'I don't want to fucking open it,' Ben was saying. 'Knowing you, it'll blow up in me face.'

Bomber was shaking his head. He was wearing the shorts that he'd worn the day before, but no shirt or vest. His tits and belly seemed to have inflated further since I last beheld them, and, for some reason, he'd fashioned a daisy-chain and wound it round his head. He looked like a down-market Roman emperor.

'It's not a trick,' said Bomber. 'It's a present. Open it.'

'Go on, Ben,' I said.

He sipped his tea moodily, and passed the package to me. 'You open it.'

I tore off the wrapping, allowing long shreds of paper to fall to the grass, to reveal a brand-new, white-and-shiny

184

bicycle pump. I gave the pump to Ben, who blinked at it dully.

'What the fuck's this?'

'It's a bike pump,' said Bomber. 'To replace the one I nicked off you when we were kids. Remember?'

Ben tutted and, with disdain, tossed the pump across the lawn.

Bomber retrieved the discarded gift, extending and contracting it to demonstrate its usefulness. 'I thought this was why you had a go at me. 'Cause I nicked your pump,' he persisted. 'So I was making a fucking, you know, peace-offering. It was meant to be, what's the word, *symbolic*.'

Ben bit into a slice of toast and said nothing. Bomber gave me a resigned look that seemed to say, 'At least I tried,' then returned to the house. I was about to appeal to Ben when we heard voices from the far end of the garden, and Malcolm and Charles appeared. They were both dripping wet and stark naked.

'The water's lovely,' said Malcolm happily, as they loped past us, their bollocks jiggling. Open-mouthed, Ben stared at their pale retreating arses. Then, turning to me, his face aghast, he said, 'See that? What did I tell you?'

At eleven a.m. we held our first group session in the garden. It was a beautiful day, with a cool breeze blowing in from the sea. We tried to start the session by holding hands, but Ben refused to join in.

'Aw, Ben,' I grumbled.

'No. Leave Ben alone,' said Vaughan graciously. 'Holding hands is not compulsory.'

I began by explaining to the others about the bicycle pump, and Bomber learned, for the first time, why my brother held a grudge against him.

'Hey, that's not on,' he complained, looking at Ben, but

185

addressing us all. 'I didn't shag Jo on Guy's behalf, you know. He did it all by his fucking self.'

Ben silently glared at Bomber.

Tentatively, Vaughan said, 'But would you not admit – and I think this is how Ben sees it – that you may still have engineered a situation in which Guy, or indeed any full-blooded male, would have found it difficult to say no?'

'Rubbish,' said Bomber. 'You can lead a man to pussy, but you can't make him shag.' Then he folded his arms and nodded to himself, as if he'd won a debate at the Oxford Union.

With a trace of irritation, Charles said, 'Actually, do you mind if we change the subject? In case it has escaped your attention, the pussy in question happens to belong to my fucking girlfriend.'

'I was there first,' affirmed Bomber.

'And I came second,' I added childishly, holding up my hand.

'It's not a competition, is it?' rebuked Vaughan.

'Excuse me,' said Ben, his brow knotted in bemusement. 'But did the big bloke . . .'

'Charles. Call me Charles,' said Charles, with a polite bow.

'Charles,' echoed Ben, as if he found the name difficult to pronounce. 'Did you just say you'd got a girlfriend?'

'Yes. The lady with whom your brother has, in the past, been all too well acquainted. Why do you ask?'

'No reason,' fibbed Ben, now deeply confused.

'He thinks you're gay,' I said.

Ben punched me on the shoulder.

'Anyway,' said Bomber manfully. 'Let's not have any more grief. If I've upset Ben, or anyone else, I'm sorry. I didn't fucking mean to.'

Nodding with satisfaction, Vaughan turned to Ben. 'Ben? How do you feel about what Bomber has just said?'

Ben shrugged. 'All right.'

'Wouldn't you agree that Bomber is being rather adult about all this?'

Grudgingly, Ben said, 'S'pose.'

Vaughan clapped his hands together. 'Good. Good! Now we're making progress!'

In the hope of building on his success, Vaughan pressed Bomber to recall the precise origin of hostilities between himself and my brother. Bomber started to tell a story about a sledge that his dad had bought for him when he was eleven.

'It cost a bomb. A real big fucker. Remember, Ben?'

Ben nodded. 'The rest of us only had shitty lumps of wood, but his dad was rich, so he had this massive fucking chromium-plated bastard.'

'More of a "sleigh" than a sledge,' emphasized Bomber, as if 'sleigh' was some kind of esoteric term, known only to fat people. 'It was snowing and all the kids went sledging in the woods. But there was one hill that no one dared slide down. That big steep bastard next to Dead Dog's Island.'

'That's the one,' agreed Ben.

Vaughan's eyes radiated fascination. You could tell that he thought he was on the verge of a major psychoanalytical breakthrough.

'Anyway, Ben dared me to sledge down this fucking hill. And I said I'd only do it if Ben got on the sledge with me.'

'Yeah.' Ben smiled in recollection. 'I didn't want to, but I was scared not to.'

'That was the moment, if you ask me, when the trouble started between me and him,' said Bomber, nodding at Ben.

'Please, tell us what happened,' urged Vaughan, leaning forward in his eagerness.

'Well, we went over the edge. Then we hit a tree stump, and Ben fell off.'

'Did you try to catch him?'

'No point,' answered Bomber. 'We were going too fast. But Ben never forgave me.'

'Why?' Vaughan was really excited now. 'What did you do wrong?'

'Dunno,' shrugged Bomber.

Vaughan clenched his fists. 'Come on. Don't stop now! What did you do that Ben didn't do?'

Bomber said, 'I s'pose I hung on.'

'Exactly!' said Vaughan. 'You *hung on*. Don't blame yourself for being stronger.'

'I don't.' Bomber frowned.

'Anyway, he isn't fucking stronger,' complained Ben. 'I just fell off.'

Turning to Ben, Vaughan said, 'And don't blame yourself for falling off!'

Charles, Malcolm and I began to clap and jeer.

'What a performance, old chap,' boomed Charles, sneering at Vaughan. 'Robert Redford would be proud of you.'

Unlike Ben and Bomber, the rest of us had seen the film *Ordinary People* and realized that Vaughan had been trying to duplicate a moment in cinematic history that is treasured by crap psychotherapists all over the world. Caught out, Vaughan turned blood-red with shame.

'Fuck this, let's go swimming,' said Bomber.

This time, everyone took their clothes off. Ben wandered about in the shallows for a while, wearing a pair of tiny black trunks that I'd swear he'd worn every summer since his sixteenth birthday. Finally, sensing that he was not, after all, in danger of being interfered with, he kicked off his trunks and dived into the icy waves.

When we were all drenched and breathless, Bomber lined us up to compare penis sizes. Had he been present, Gordon would have won this contest, foreskin-down. In his absence, Charles was voted the winner, with Ben second, and Bomber and I occupying equal third place. Surprisingly, it was Vaughan, not Malcolm, who came last. Vaughan found this decision difficult to accept. 'It's the cold water that's done it,' he griped, trying to wank a bit of life into himself. 'I'm usually miles bigger than this.'

He was not to be consoled, even though he won first prize in the hairy anus competition, and came a close second in the pissing-up-a-cliff contest.

Ben, on the other hand, was pretty pleased to own the second-biggest dick, especially with Bomber as judge. He suddenly dropped his 'don't-fuck-with-me' act and relaxed. It's amazing what a little penile pride can do for a man. When we all sat down in a circle and held hands, Ben clasped me and Bomber without restraint.

'Let's focus our energy,' said Vaughan.

'Yeah,' said Bomber. 'Size isn't important.'

For some reason, this made everyone whoop with laughter, including Vaughan. We passed around bottles of beer and began to drink. Everyone talked at once. Ben and Bomber sang 'Chain Gang' by Sam Cooke, with the rest of us providing the 'Oohs' and the 'Ahs'.

We whiled away the afternoon in this pleasant, irresponsible way, sitting on the beach, naked and unsightly, steadily getting drunk. Then Malcolm started crying.

'I want to say something,' he sniffed.

'Whatsisname wants to say something,' said Vaughan.

'I want to say that as I don't drink alcohol, I feel rather left out. I feel that no one is interested in me.'

At this, Ben and Bomber rolled about, laughing and holding their sides.

Charles said, 'No. Not right to laugh. Let's play the "trust" game. Malcolm needs the "trust" game.'

We stood in a circle, with Malcolm in the centre, his eyes tightly closed. Malcolm allowed himself to flop, and we hurled him from one set of arms to another, shouting

189

'Wheee!' each time we did so. After thirty seconds, without warning, Vaughan deliberately lowered his arms and allowed Malcolm to crash to earth.

'Ow! Ow!' cried Malcolm, clutching his back and writhing on the pebbles. 'That bloody well hurt!'

'Vaughan, you did that deliberately,' I said, while the others sniggered.

Vaughan pleaded guilty with a sad little bow of his head.

'Bit uncalled-for, wasn't it?' said Charles as Bomber, still laughing, helped Malcolm to his feet.

'I couldn't help myself,' said Vaughan, matter-of-fact. 'He *hasn't* got a bigger one than me. I won't have it. *Mine's* bigger.'

Malcolm was so upset that he went back to the house and shut himself in his room. After tea Ben came to me and suggested that he and I take Malcolm out to cheer him up. 'There's a pub down the road that we could go to. He can't help being gay, can he? It's a shame for the bloke.'

While Charles, Bomber and Vaughan stayed in the garden, smoking Bomber's dope, Ben and I set off with Malcolm. The pub, The Captain's Biscuit, was within walking distance, at the end of a long, narrow country lane lined by high hedgerows. We arrived as darkness was falling, and were served by a stony-faced landlady who narrowed her eyes at the sight of Ben's tattooed biceps. Then we settled in the corner of a dark back room.

Malcolm confided in us. 'I think the group's finished,' he admitted.

'No,' I said.

'Yes. It's over, Guy.' Malcolm's glasses were starting to look emotional again. 'The world is changing. We're already supposed to be in the post-feminist era, but in reality we're living in the no-longer-give-a-shit era. Can't you see it? Even Vaughan's lost the way.'

'Oh, forget him,' said Ben. 'He's just jealous 'cause you're only little, and you've got a bigger dick than him.'

Malcolm nodded vigorously. 'Exactly. And that's why I know it's over. Vaughan *was* this group. He never used to worry about the size of his sex organs. He was our soul and our conscience; the man who held us together. If he doesn't care any more, then who does?'

Unable to profess to any personal interest in the matter, I said, 'You care, Malcolm.'

'Yes, but that's because I'm the only one of us who *needs* this group. The rest of you have got friends. I've got nobody, really.'

At this, Malcolm hung his head and sobbed. The pub was full of customers, many of whom turned to stare. While feeling sorry for Malcolm, Ben and I were also greatly embarrassed to be seen with him. On the pretext of collecting our empty glasses, the surly landlady walked over to the table and murmured, 'This kind of thing isn't good for business, you know.'

'He's upset,' I reasoned.

'He's a grown man,' she snapped back. 'Can't he control himself?'

Ben, ever the diplomat, said, 'Fuck off, you nasty old bag.'

This struck us all as an opportune moment to leave. We walked back in the dark, trying to cheer Malcolm all the way. By the time the lights of the house came in sight, he seemed to have accepted the idea that Vaughan, like anyone else, was imperfect and therefore entitled to the odd exhibition of human weakness.

We knocked on the front door and received no answer. The windows of the room above, Bomber's bedroom, were wide open, casting golden light on to the path. But the house lay silent and when we called, no one answered.

'Surely they can't be in bed?' I said. 'It's far too early.'

We wandered around to the back garden, but there was

no one there, and the kitchen door and french windows were also locked. The lower floor of the house was in darkness. We started shouting. After a few moments, Bomber's face appeared at an upstairs window. He looked surprised to see us. 'Hey, Malcolm, Vaughan wants you. Go round to the front.'

Before we could ask him what he was talking about, he withdrew his head.

Puzzled, we returned to the front of the house. Malcolm, leading the way, hammered on the door. Suddenly, Ben shouted a warning. Glancing up at the windows of Bomber's room, I saw what Ben had seen: two bare arses perched on the sill. Then, noiselessly, something dropped out of the arse on the right and landed on Malcolm. Malcolm put his hand up to his hair, inspected his hand and shrieked, realizing that there was a fresh, warm turd on his head.

There was a chorus of cheers from the window above, and Bomber's face appeared between the stereo bare bottoms. 'Got the bastard!' he roared.

Ben and I couldn't help laughing. It isn't every day that you see a man wearing a turd. Charles, the arse on the left, had climbed back into the room and was now cackling and pointing down at the shit-stained Malcolm. Vaughan, owner of the winning sphincter, was still seated on the sill. Giggling maniacally, he half-turned to admire his marksmanship. Instead of weeping, as one might have reasonably expected him to do, Malcolm began to scream and shake his fist in furious outrage, and the sight of this made Vaughan laugh so much that he lurched backwards.

Then he fell out of the window.

The Sapient Sexists

Malcolm had been right. That was the end of our men's group. Malcolm could not bring himself to forgive Vaughan for shitting on his head, and Vaughan, who had broken his arm in the fall from the window, was unable to forgive any of us for laughing at him more than we'd laughed at Malcolm.

From my point of view, the weekend in Devon had been utterly disastrous. It was true that Ben had made progress: he had held hands and bathed naked with other men, as well as making his peace with Bomber. But the group had fallen apart before we'd had a chance to work on his violent tendencies.

As for Bomber, he had indeed cried. But only with laughter, at the sight of Vaughan on the ground, being kicked by a man with a turd on his head. And he was no closer to accepting the basic tenets of feminism than Bob Hope, the Pope, or a bar of soap.

I had failed. I now realized that I didn't have a chance in Crouch End of fulfilling Natalie's sacred tasks, and that my only remaining hope lay in deceiving her. In theory, of course, I'd renounced deception, but honesty wasn't doing me much good, either. And I wanted to hold that woman in my arms so badly that it was making my teeth itch. Do you know the sensation I mean? If not, good luck to you: you're probably a well-balanced individual.

Ben dropped me off at Shepley Drive late on Sunday

evening. The house was dark and still. A note from Natalie lay waiting for me on the kitchen table.

> 6 p.m. Sunday
> Guy: Hope the weekend went well. Have gone out. Won't be back until late. Erik is with your mum and dad.
>
> Natalie.

This troubled me. She'd mentioned nothing about a night out to me, and I wondered, darkly, where she was and, more importantly, who might be fucking her. I walked out to the garage and felt sick when I saw that the Mini had gone. Returning to the house, I took a beer from the fridge and started pacing up and down like an expectant father, or, more accurately, an expectant cuckold.

Absurdly, I left the house to patrol the pavement in front of the driveway. Every time a set of headlights blazed round the corner, I thought it might be the Mini returning home. But it was always a different car, going home to someone else's house, and I felt the way you feel when you're thirteen and the girl you've arranged to meet outside the cinema hasn't shown, and every girl approaching in the distance starts to look like the girl you're waiting for, the only girl who's stayed at home.

By about two, I got bored. The sick feeling in my gut had intensified, but so had my exhaustion. I re-entered the house, went up to Natalie's room and turned on the light. Her sweet fragrance filled the air. The tarot cards that she'd inherited from her mother were resting on the cabinet beside her bed. I opened the box, tipping the cards out on to the quilt. After shuffling the twenty-two trumps, I asked who-ever was listening, whoever gave a toss, about my prospects of winning Natalie's love. And I wasn't in the slightest bit surprised when I turned over a card showing a black, crowned skeleton and read the word 'Death'.

I picked Erik up from my mum's in the morning. Natalie came home in the early afternoon. She was carrying her violin case and a bunch of vivid red roses. My first question to her was, 'Who gave you the flowers?'

Dropping the violin and the roses on the sofa, she reached over and took the baby from me. 'They're from Rob. Rob Mitchell? I played at the Verandah last night. The Keepers were heading the bill. They needed a violinist at short notice.'

'Having heard their last record, I'd say they needed a guitarist, a drummer, a bassist, a keyboard player and a fucking singer.'

Patting Erik's back, she said, 'What are you getting so worked up about?'

'Guess.'

'I've no idea.'

'You've been out *all night*.'

She laughed. 'You were out all weekend. So fucking what?'

'Natalie, what's going on?'

'Er, sorry Guy.' Her eyes glittered in warning. 'Perhaps it's slipped your mind, but you're only a guest in this house. You're here to help look after Erik and carry out the tasks I've set for you. Knowing where I am, who I'm with and what I'm doing with them is *not* part of the deal.'

I felt the need to retaliate. 'The guys in my group think you and your tasks are a pile of shit, Natalie. They think you're just out to humiliate me.'

Her eyes seared through me. 'And what do *you* think, Guy?'

'I think your sister was a lot nicer than you.'

Her eyes softened. She placed a protective hand over the

195

back of the baby's head. 'Gina was a lot nicer than either of us.'

I spent the rest of the day wondering why I was wasting my time on this frosty, wilful woman. But at dusk she called me into the bathroom while she was submerged in the tub. I took one look at her and stopped wondering.

'You haven't told me how you got on at the weekend.'

'It was great. Really,' I answered guiltily.

She began to soap her right leg, probably with the deliberate intention of torturing me. 'Go on,' she prompted.

I hesitated. 'Aren't we supposed to discuss this in front of the shrine?'

'No. I can't be bothered with all that any more. Tell me now.'

'Well, it went remarkably well. Bomber cried.'

'Really?'

'Yeah. He really did. Isn't that great?'

'I don't know, yet. What made him cry?'

'Oh, Ben kissed him and, er, Bomber was really moved.'

'Ben kissed Bomber?'

'Yes, and then Ben said that he knew that violence achieved nothing, and promised not to solve problems with his fists ever again.'

For a seasoned liar, I was doing extremely badly. I could tell that Natalie thought so too. She was staring at me in sullen scepticism. 'I see. As easy as that, was it?'

'Yes,' I said. 'Amazing, really. Who'd have believed it?'

Her expression hardened. 'Not me, for a start.' She rinsed herself. 'And what about Bomber's lessons in feminism?'

I swallowed audibly. 'Great. Couldn't have gone better.'

She sniffed. 'Yeah, let me guess: I'll bet you made a major breakthrough there, too. I'll bet he admitted that his attitude to women was founded on the three main patriarchal principles: intimidation, domination and subjugation. Then he promised never to degrade women again with his base and dehumanizing desires. Am I right?'

'Well, yes,' I said, cautiously. 'Words to that effect.'

'Pass me a towel.'

I handed her a fluffy white bath towel. She pulled out the plug, stood up in the water and stared into my eyes. 'Guy, if I find out that you're lying, you realize it'll be all over between us?'

I thought that I'd heard this somewhere before. 'Isn't that a line from a film?'

'Don't push your luck,' she said. She climbed out of the bath, her skin glistening and I stepped back, repelled by her overpowering aura.

'So what happens now?' I asked humbly.

'You and your friends are invited to a dinner party, on the eighteenth of August. Does that date mean anything to you?'

'I'm not sure,' I said.

'It should do. It's your wedding anniversary.'

I closed my eyes in self-reproach. 'Oh, shit.'

'Yes,' she said. 'How many weeks has she been dead? And you've forgotten already.'

'No, that's not fair. I used to forget when she was alive.'

'You say that a lot, don't you?'

'What?'

'"That's not fair." You're always going on about "fairness", aren't you? It sounds funny, really, coming from someone as unfair as you.'

I glanced down at her tits.

'And stop looking at my tits.'

'Sorry.'

'So, to recap: we meet at eight o'clock sharp on the eighteenth of August, on the upper floor of the Nutbarn restaurant in Stockport. I want to see them all: Bomber, Ben and Jo. Bomber and Ben are to arrive holding hands. Over dinner, me and a hand-picked panel of judges will ask you and the other guests questions. And you'd better be prepared, Guy. Because you won't get a second chance.'

I informed Ben, Bomber and Jo of the date of the dinner. Bomber, as usual, warmly accepted my invitation. 'I'll be there, mate. You can count on me. Should be a right fucking laugh. I'll get the wife to give me a few tips. She knows a bit about Women's Lib . . .'

'Feminism. It hasn't been called Women's Lib for years.'

'Well, whatever. It's all about respecting women, and women respecting 'emselves. Am I right?'

Heartened, I said, 'Yeah. Yeah. You're right . . .'

Ben claimed to have an important darts match on the appointed night, but when I pleaded with him, he promised to find some other working-class illiterate to lob missiles at a board in his stead.

Jo now lived with Charles in his half-a-house in Sale. Impressed by the awful gravity of my situation, he offered to ferry Jo to the meal, and to brief her beforehand on the rudiments of sexual politics. Only when he'd put the phone down did it occur to me that Charles himself had never demonstrated the barest understanding of sexual politics.

At seven p.m. on the day of my doom, Ben and I met Jo and Charles in a Stockport bar. The pub, situated on Little Underbank, had the suspicious name of The Happy Camper. At the sight of Jo, Ben became foolish and tongue-tied and kept spilling his pint. He'd been ready to despise her; she was, after all, the harlot that had tempted me away from his beloved Gina. But face to face with this ravishing, gentle vision, his ire was flushed away by a torrent of schoolboy ardour.

'Got lotsa tattoos, aincha?' she remarked.

Ben flushed proudly. 'Oh, yeah, yeah, yeah.'

'Bet they 'urt a bit, dint they?'

'Yeah, yeah, yeah.'

Charles, forced into the role of jealous, disapproving chaperon, interrupted this lofty metaphysical discourse to say, 'What's sexual harassment, Jo?'

'Oh, yeah.' She placed her orange juice on a beer mat, and stared straight ahead, struggling to remember her lines. 'Sexual 'arassment commonly occurs in the workplace, and hinvolves hundermining women and their heffectiveness, usually by the persistent use of sexual hinnuendo and suggestive . . . suggestive . . .'

Charles sighed. 'Body language.'

'Body language. 'Arassment may hencompass anyfink from haddressing a female colleague as "love" or "sweetheart", to houtright sexual assault.'

'Hey!' I enthused. 'Well done, Jo.'

'All right,' she cautioned. 'Yer don't need to patronize me.'

Surprised, I said, 'Good point. Sorry.'

'Patron,' she resumed. 'A word derived from the Latin *Patronus*. Not to be confused, hof course, with *patriarcha*, meaning the 'ead of a clan, horigin of the word patriarchy, meaning an houtmoded system hof fellacentric government.'

Ben and I applauded.

'Well done, darling,' oozed Charles. 'Just one teensy criticism . . . the word is *phallocentric*.'

'Why? What did I say?'

'You said "fella". As in man. When you should have said "phallo". As in sweaty prick.'

Jo looked confused. 'Same fing, innit?'

'Ben?' I prompted.

'I renounce violence,' he replied wearily.

'What do you renounce?'

'Violence. How many more times?'

Bomber arrived, dressed in an evening suit. The rest of us were attired in what a nightclub bouncer might have described as "smart casual-wear". He turned pale at the sight of us. 'You fucking twat, Lockheart! You told me it was a dinner party.'

'It is,' I said. 'An informal dinner party.'

Annoyed, he tore off his bow-tie and threw it at me. 'I had to hire this fucking suit from Moss Bros. You can fucking well pay for it, now.'

'OK. Relax,' I said. 'What are you drinking?'

My mouth was dry as I led Bomber, Ben and Jo up a dark staircase to the hired room above the Nutbarn. We'd left Charles behind in the pub. He didn't need to hang around at all, but I think he was understandably afraid of leaving Jo alone with three men who fancied her, especially as two of them had already 'ram-raided her pussy'.

Half-way up the stairs, I halted and turned to brief my troops. Jo was behind me, followed by Ben, then Bomber. 'OK. One more thing. Don't ask me why, but we've got to go in there holding hands . . .'

Ben raised a token protest, but I could tell he didn't really mind, as this gave him an opportunity to get closer to Jo. Bomber, being a bit of a slut, didn't give a fuck whose hand he held. And so it came to pass that Natalie's final demand was met, relatively painlessly.

Like a chain-gang comprised entirely of public-spirited volunteers, we sidled through the door at the top of the stairs and found ourselves in a swept, bare-boarded attic. Through an open window came the chatter and drone of a busy Stockport street. Two long tables, formed from boards and trestles, lined the walls on either side of the window, enabling the guests to face their hosts and still be separated by a distance of about twelve feet.

There were five places at the women's table, and in the centre sat a figure that I recognized as Natalie, wearing a white wedding dress and a long veil. I hadn't seen the dress before, and wondered where it had come from. Rose hadn't kept her wedding dress, not wishing to be reminded of her husband, and Gina had been married in leathers and Doc Martens.

On Natalie's left lurked Les Bean's friends, the two shorn sisters, one of whom was pleasant-faced and self-contained, the other bespectacled, narrow-lipped and nervy. On the far right sat Beany herself. At close quarters, her face resembled an intelligent shovel.

But next to Natalie, in the place of honour, was someone I had hoped never to see again: my old enemy. She of the self-righteous scowl and the awesome moustache: the formidable Anne Fermesky. At the sight of her, all my hopes withered away, because I knew that Anne's presence was a sure indication of the contempt in which Natalie held me.

'Hey! Is it fancy dress, or what?' laughed Bomber, indicating the silent bride. The sisters did not respond. 'Yeah, fancy dress,' he said, trying again. 'As you can see, I've come as a fat bastard!' Then he glanced at Anne Fermesky, who was eyeing him with intense dislike and added, 'No offence.'

Attempting to camouflage this *faux-pas*, I let go of Jo and headed for the women's table with my hand held out in greeting. 'Hiya, everybody . . .'

'Please,' said Les, exposing her palms as if to push me away. 'No physical contact. Guests are requested to keep to their own table.'

Bemused, we took our places and stared grimly across the room as Bean took care of the introductions. 'I'm Lesley, although I prefer "Lee". This is Amanda (pleasant face), and this is Freddy (miserable with glasses). Natalie, you know, of course, and, by special invitation, we also have a very famous writer with us. She's taken time off from a busy book-signing schedule to be here today, and I think we should all put our hands together to welcome the inimitable *Anne Fermesky*!'

The sisters clapped enthusiastically, and we sexists joined in, our spirits weighed down by a powerful sense of imminent castration. Anne bowed her surly head, her jowls wobbling slightly as she did so.

Anne's latest masterpiece, incidentally, attacked the concept of 'the sanitized woman', who obscures her natural feminine odours with perfume and soap. The book, entitled *Women Who Wash Too Much*, formed the final part of the 'Proud Sister' trilogy, following on from *Sister be Fat, Sister be Proud* and *Sister be Brave, Don't Have a Shave*. One day, no doubt, Anne's publishers will issue all three books together in one volume, under the title *Sister be Grubby, Hairy and Tubby*.

Bomber, whose profession had accustomed him to polite hypocrisy, arose and began to introduce everyone on our table, but was cut short by Fermesky, who said, 'Yes, we know who *you* are.'

Infuriatingly, this undistinguished burst of rudeness reduced the occupants of the far table to fits of the giggles. The situation looked grave, and I sensed that things were destined to get worse before they got *a lot* worse.

Two waitresses from the restaurant downstairs brought up a set three-course vegetarian dinner of lentil soup, aubergine bake and apple pie, served with either ice cream or soya seagull-droppings. One of the waitresses asked if we needed anything else, and Bomber, unfamiliar with vegetarian cuisine, said, 'How about some food?'

The Nutbarn restaurant had no licence to serve alcohol, so Beany Shovel-Face had provided organic wine at her own expense. We ate in uneasy silence, all drinking to excess because of tension, while opposite us Natalie's friends chattered happily among themselves. But although Natalie occasionally nodded her head in response to a companion's question, she neither spoke nor raised her veil to eat or drink.

After we'd eaten, and the table had been cleared, Bean said, 'John Lancaster, would you please rise?'

'Oh, fuck,' grumbled Bomber. 'Do I have to? I'm pissed.'

'We'd prefer you to stand,' said Amanda, sweetly.

Reluctantly, he acceded to her request.

'Now,' said Bean. 'We don't want you to feel under any pressure. This applies to all of you. We just want to know whether Guy has done what he claims to have done. So, John, in your own words, please: perhaps you could tell us what you understand the term "feminism" to mean?'

Without hesitation, he replied, 'Well, as far as I can make out, it all comes down to respect.' He glanced at me. I gave him a nod of encouragement. 'Women showing respect for 'emselves, and men, well, showing respect for women.'

The sisters exchanged surprised glances.

'All right,' pursued Bean. 'And how might men show respect for women, do you think?'

'Lots of ways.'

'Could you give me an example?'

A concentration cleft appeared at the bridge of his nose. 'Well, when a lady walks up to a door, a man should hold it open for her.'

The women rocked with laughter.

Bomber was perspiring. 'Oh. Sorry. Not just ladies ... you should hold the door open for any woman, even if she looks like a slag.'

More laughter, and a loud sigh. The sigh was provided by me, by the way.

'I see,' said Les. 'Has it not occurred to you that a feminist, or even a "slag", might be capable of opening this hypothetical door all by herself?'

'Yeah, but hang on a mo',' chided Bomber, shaking a plump forefinger. 'What if she's old and knackered-in? Some of these swing-doors can be pretty lethal, you know ...'

Under my breath I hissed, 'I thought your wife was giving you lessons?'

He leaned over Ben to speak to me. 'She did. She said that Women's Lib is when the bird gets doors held open for her, instead of the bird having to hold doors open for blokes. Also, it's somethin' to do with burning bras. So the wife says, anyway.'

'OK. What's a "post-feminist?" asked Fermesky, making notes.

Bomber scratched his arse reflectively. 'S'pose it's a feminist who works for the Royal fucking Mail.'

The wimmin were falling about now, and even wretched-unto-death Fermesky was smiling.

'What about crying?' said Fermesky. 'We've been led to believe that you attended a men's group, and unleashed your repressed emotions. Is that true?'

Bomber nodded, his jaw tightening. I could tell that he'd reached the end of his tether.

'Could you cry for us now?' sneered Fermesky.

'Only if you sat on me,' retorted Bomber, to sniggers from Ben. There were no sniggers from me, dear friend. I was too busy witnessing my own execution.

Fermesky sighed and jotted Bomber's remark down, ready to use it as evidence on the Day of Judgement, if God turned out to be a fat woman with a moustache.

Next, Bean asked Ben to rise.

'Fuck off,' he said.

'I beg your pardon?'

'Fuck off.'

'Are you refusing to stand?'

'No. I'm telling you to fuck off.'

'You've been described as a violent male . . .'

'Fuck off.'

'Have you any comment to make about that?'

'Yes. Fuck off.'

Bomber was now convulsed with laughter, and, once again, tears were rolling down his cheeks. Sweet Jo, sensitive enough to realize how badly things were going for me, reached over to pat my hand.

'Benjamin James Lockheart, do you renounce violence?'

'Fuck off.'

'Have you anything to say apart from "Fuck off"?'

'How about "Fuck off, ugly"?' suggested Bomber, cackling.

Giving up, Bean seated herself. Ben turned to me and smiled sadly, as if to say, 'Believe me, this is all for the best.'

With belligerent triumph, fat Anne turned to the other women and said, 'Well? That's it, isn't it? Lockheart has failed. He's been utterly discredited. Why carry on?'

Patiently, Amanda said, 'No. We're to reserve judgement until the end of the trial. Isn't that right, Natalie?'

The bogus bride nodded.

'Next we have the dramatic interlude,' explained Bean. 'Then we talk to Josephine, then we cross-examine the suspected sexist.'

'They're all sexists,' objected Fermesky. 'You only have to look at them.'

(What do you call ten thousand Anne Fermeskys lying dead at the bottom of the sea? Not enough. What do you call Anne Fermesky lying? Anne Fermesky. What do you call Anne Fermesky? *Not enough*.)

Amanda, still smiling like a lady mayoress in the presence of a member of the royal family, said, 'Invited guests, for your entertainment, we are now pleased to present a dramatic interlude. Please welcome the women of the Eager Beaver Theatre Company, who will perform for us a one-act play, loosely adapted from a fairy tale by the Brothers Grimm and entitled *The Rightful Bride* . . .'

To cheers and applause from the reconstructed table, two women skipped in, one dressed like Cinderella, the other

205

looking like Dick Whittington. Both players wore silvery masks that covered their entire faces.

Acting as narrator, Amanda began to read from a thin script. 'There was once a poor peasant girl who lived in the forest. She was beautiful and wise, and spent her spare time researching gender studies.'

(The actor in the dress mimed assiduous study, while Ben and Bomber, friends at last, sniggered with childish glee.)

'One day, a handsome prince rode by and saw her sitting in the forest, reading. Transfixed by her beauty, he said, "Come away to my palace and be my bride."'

(By way of illustration, the actor-dressed-as-Whittington knelt down before the peasant girl and did some serious beseeching.)

'The peasant girl said, "Thanks for the offer, but I need my own space at the moment. I'm trying to recover my selfhood, you see."

'But alas! When the peasant girl was *au fait* with all the issues and had learned to embrace her own positive and negative emotions, she found that the handsome prince no longer wanted her. In fact, he repeatedly passed her by in the forest without appearing to recognize her. Then news came that the prince was engaged to be married to another woman.

'On the day of the wedding, the peasant girl took out her dead grandmother's wedding dress and put it on. Then she sneaked into the royal palace, security in those days being somewhat lax.'

(At this point in the action, the peasant girl went to sit in Natalie's chair, and Natalie the bride stood before the prince.)

'Then the prince, wondering who this guest might be, said, "Please. Take off your veil that I might gaze upon your face . . ."'

Slowly, Natalie unpinned her long white veil and bared her head. Then I saw that her once-long hair had been cropped close to her scalp. Her face was free of make-up. She had made herself look exactly like Gina, and this act of premeditated cruelty made me gasp. Overwhelmed, I stood and walked towards her. Natalie turned to face me, as Amanda intoned the last line of the story:

'And then the scales seemed to fall from his eyes, and he recognized his rightful bride.'

Before I could speak, Ben released a deafening, agonized roar. Then he completely lost control, overturning tables and smashing plates, so that Bomber and I had to use all our strength to restrain him.

The Sweetest Sexist

I spent the night on Ben's sofa. It seemed the only sensible thing to do. I was disgusted by Natalie's behaviour, and by the way that it had affected Ben. Yet the thought of not having her in my life any more made me feel physically sick.

In the morning I looked after Sam and the baby while Ben and Rachel went to the supermarket. At noon I went to Natalie's house. I knew that there was no longer any hope for us, but I needed to hear her say it, in her own words, in her own beloved voice.

There was a powder-blue Porsche parked in the drive. Water was sploshing out of a drain-pipe into a grid. I guessed that Natalie was taking a shower. Quietly, I admitted myself to the house. An unfamiliar leather jacket was draped over the bannister rail in the hall. Seized by a terrible foreboding, I climbed the stairs. There was an open sports bag on the landing, and a heap of discarded clothing. The bathroom door was ajar, and I could hear a voice, a man's voice, humming merrily within. Gently, I pushed open the door.

The man was naked, with his back towards me. Through a veil of steam, I could see dirty reddish-brown fuzz sprouting from his thighs, his shoulders and the cleft of his hollow buttocks. His right foot rested on the rim of the bath, and he was mopping his foot and ankle with a towel. Sensing my presence, he turned to face me.

Although he wasn't wearing his glasses, I instantly recognized his beard. It was Rob Mitchell. And rather than looking startled or bashful, as any decent person would have done, Mitchell simply bared his long, off-white teeth in an approximation of a smile and offered his hand in greeting.

'Oh, hello there. It's Guy, isn't it?'

'What are you doing here?'

Still smiling, he said, 'What does it look like?'

Appalled, I stared down at his privates and saw that Mitchell had an extraordinarily small dick. A dick that would have made poor Vaughan look like a stallion. Worse still, there was a fat red pimple growing near the tip of Rob's knob.

'Ugh,' I said.

'Come, now,' he said. 'Let's not be childish about this.'

'Who's being childish? Fuck off, out of my house!'

Natalie walked in to find out what all the noise was about. She was carrying Erik and wearing only her underwear.

'Right. What's going on?' she demanded.

'You tell me!' I fumed.

I tried to cover the baby's eyes. I wanted to protect him from the sight of Mitchell's nakedness, having read somewhere that traumas encountered in the first few years of life can cause permanent psychic damage.

Mitchell wrapped the towel around himself and squeezed past us.

'Rob?' said Natalie. 'Where are you going?'

With undeniable aplomb, he stooped to gather up his belongings from the landing.

'You don't have to go,' said Natalie. 'This is my house.'

'It's not your fucking house!' I snapped. 'Half of this house was Gina's, and, legally, what was hers is mine.'

'We'll see about that,' she threatened, through clenched teeth. 'Rob? Rob?'

Carrying his belongings, Mitchell started to descend the

stairs. 'Leave me out of this,' he said, without glancing back. 'This is between you and him.'

After Mitchell's departure, I made some coffee. Natalie and I met to glower at each other over the kitchen table. But I found that I couldn't look into her eyes and think at the same time. As I've already mentioned, staring people out was a speciality of hers.

'Well? Did you fuck him?' I said.

'That's my business.'

My stomach churned, because I fancied that I could smell Mitchell on her.

'But why him?' I said, trying to keep my voice steady. 'I mean, I understand why you're sick of me. I'm sick of you, too. Especially after last night. But what the fuck do you see in that ugly little creep?'

'Firstly, I don't have to account for my actions to you. And, secondly, he isn't ugly.'

'Natalie, he's got a face like a cunt, even down to the V-shaped beard.'

'I'm not prepared to discuss it. Just look for somewhere else to live, Guy.'

'Why should I? Half this house is mine . . .'

She smirked and folded her arms.

I was incensed by her nonchalance. 'Do you want me to go to a solicitor?'

'Do what you have to do.'

'Now you're quoting *Kramer Versus Kramer*! What's the matter with you, lately? Everything you say sounds like a line from a fucking film! Why can't you just sit down and talk to me, like any normal person?'

She wouldn't answer.

'Natalie, we've got a baby. We've got a baby and I love you, you silly cow. Doesn't that count for anything?'

Averting her eyes, she gazed down serenely at her outstretched fingers. I felt like crying, but stopped myself. I felt that I'd been submissive enough for one lifetime. I got up, tipped the remains of my coffee into the sink and walked out.

Later, it occurred to me that Natalie's affair with the newsreader was yet another test, which I had failed with flying colours. In many ways it was the ultimate test: *did I think that Natalie was my personal possession?* Yes, I did. I believed that she belonged to me, body and soul.

And now that Natalie knew this about me, I had nothing left to lose.

I borrowed my father's megaphone, the instrument with which, before his retirement, my decent left-wing dad had addressed his union comrades. Over the years, this loud-hailer had reasoned with brutish policemen, pleaded with blackleg printers, commiserated with jobless miners. But tonight I had a different use for it.

I drove to the dank, squalid part of Manchester where that tight-arse Mitchell had converted a disused warehouse into a night club. I parked the mini in a back street, and lifted dad's megaphone out of the boot.

The Verandah was not due to open for another fifteen minutes, but there was already a sizeable queue of pale, unhealthy patrons leading up to its sturdy entrance. A band called Last Orders was supporting The Final Solution, and every tone-deaf depressive within a thirty-mile radius had turned up for the event. Leaning against a lamp-post, facing the club, I turned on the megaphone and addressed the gathering revellers.

'Now hear this. Now hear this,' I began, unpromisingly. 'This club is owned by Rob Mitchell. Rob Mitchell is not hip. Rob Mitchell is a newsreader.'

Encouragingly, most of the people in the queue started to laugh. Mitchell was widely disliked, especially by the bands on his record label, some of whom wondered how they

211

could sell thousands of records and yet still receive no royalties. But the patrons of Mitchell's club preferred to give money to a certified tosspot than run the risk of not being there, and therefore being square.

'Rob Mitchell has a very small penis,' I continued, to cheers from the spectators. 'Upon that penis, he has a pimple. That pimple is twice as big as the penis itself. Last night, despite the fact that he has a lovely blonde wife in Knutsford, Mitchell inserted his pimple-dick into my girl-friend. Now, before you enter this club, let me ask you a question. Do you really want to give your money to an adulterous newsreader with a diseased cock?'

The double doors to the Verandah opened. Two large black bouncers peered out at me and I glimpsed Mitchell himself, hovering behind them, tight-lipped and tense.

'I repeat, Rob Mitchell has a minuscule dick. It would not look out of place on a three-year-old, or a young gerbil.'

After consulting Mitchell, one of the bouncers walked over to confront me. He was broad-shouldered and guard-edly vicious. 'Would you mind moving along, please?' he said, in a quiet, high-pitched voice. He was dying to hit me.

'Rob Mitchell is not hip, has never been hip, and never will be hip,' I repeated. 'Rob Mitchell is a newsreader.'

Not knowing what else to do, the bouncer shoved me, and the people in the queue shouted out their disapproval. 'Now hear this,' I said. 'Rob Mitchell is a not-very-well-endowed newsreader.'

Someone signalled to the bouncer from the doorway, and he ran back inside. I continued to broadcast for another few minutes, until a police patrol car rolled up alongside me. Two uniformed officers left the car and took away my megaphone. One of them was tall, the other my height, with a crew cut.

Mitchell came out to talk to them. He was gratifyingly

flustered. 'This man has been threatening me and harassing my customers,' he lied. 'I want him arrested.'

The police officers listened calmly to both sides of the story. Eventually the tall one turned to me and said, 'Do you promise to stop making a nuisance of yourself, sir?'

'No,' I replied.

His skinhead colleague sighed. 'Then I'm afraid we're going to have to arrest you.'

By this time, the Verandah had officially opened. The freaks shuffling through its doors had lost all interest in me and my megaphone. Mitchell smirked at me in womanly triumph as I was guided into the back of the police car. The car pulled away, and I saw him turn and step jauntily back into the club, rubbing his hands together with satisfaction.

But as soon as we'd rounded the corner, the two police officers started laughing. 'Has he really got a little dick?' asked the tall one.

'Microscopic,' I said, laughing with them.

'Thought so,' said the one with the crew cut. 'He looks the type. You can always tell.'

They stopped the car, and, after removing the batteries, returned my father's megaphone.

'We're not arresting you,' said the tall one. 'Just don't cause any more bother.'

'No,' I said. 'I mean, I won't.'

'Don't let life get you down,' said the skinhead. 'Nothing's worth worrying about. If you worry, you'll end up bald, like me.'

'Yeah,' said his friend. 'But we're sorry about your girlfriend.'

'Thanks,' I said, opening the car door.

'Take care, now,' said the skinhead. Then they drove away, leaving me standing on the pavement, holding a megaphone.

213

This show of consideration from these two officers of the law nearly broke my heart, convincing me that the world was a deeply confused and confusing place, where our loved ones could destroy us, and our supposed enemies could humble us with unsolicited acts of kindness.

Weeping, I wandered into a gay pub near Piccadilly station and got horribly drunk. I dimly recall being held over a wash-basin in the gents by a nice man with a moustache, while I puked up several pints of beer, then reeling to the station with the vague intention of catching the last train home. It wasn't that I didn't want to drink and drive. I was simply too drunk to remember where I'd parked my car.

I arrived at the station, but the last train had gone. I went outside to wait in the rain for a taxi, then placed my hands in my pockets, only to discover that I had no money.

I began to walk home. Every so often, the occupants of passing cars, all of whom seemed to possess the same round, red Mancunian face, honked their horns or rolled down their windows to shout incoherent abuse. You'd think that none of them had ever seen a drunk carrying a megaphone before.

One of these rowdies was disquietingly persistent. He cruised the kerb beside me, shouting and whistling. I avoided glancing in the lout's direction, lest he mistake my squint-eyed incomprehension for aggression. Eventually, I heard a car door slam. I steeled myself, expecting trouble. A hand touched my arm, and I yanked my arm away, turned and saw my brother standing there. He was smiling.

In my surprise, I lurched sideways. He caught me before I fell. 'Hello, dickhead,' he said.

'Ah, great, great,' I slurred, slapping him on the shoulder. 'Good to see you, mate. I couldn't get a train.'

'Are you surprised?' he said, helping me into his third-hand Mercedes. 'It's two o'clock in the fucking morning.'

He helped me into my seat-belt and grinned at me. 'What's the megaphone in aid of, Guy?' He took it off me and, laughing, pretended to speak into it. 'Now hear this. Now hear this. You are a stupid twat.'

'I know,' I said. 'I know I am.'

The car sped away into the traffic. 'Natalie rang me,' he explained.

'How did she sound?'

'Same as she always sounds. Like a miserable stuck-up bitch. She said you'd been making a nuisance of yourself outside the Verandah. I went to pick you up, but you weren't there. I've been driving round for the past hour trying to find you, you great tit.'

I told him about my broadcast to the nation, and the two policemen who'd laughed at the idea of a grown man with a little boy's dick. Ben couldn't stop laughing. We were driving through Levenshulme. Kate Bush was playing on the car stereo.

Cushioned from embarrassment by drink, I suddenly said, 'I love you, Ben.'

'Oh, fuck off,' he answered.

'No,' I slurred. 'I love you, mate. I really mean it.'

He laughed rudely. 'And I mean it, too. Fuck off, you big girl. What do you think this is? Oprah Winfrey?'

Although it was late, the streets were teeming with people. We stopped at a set of traffic lights and heard the sound of screaming. At first we thought it was nothing, just some girl who'd had too much to drink. But when we glanced back, we saw a guy with a dark beard dragging a woman along by her hair. He was holding a blade to her throat and shouting. She was screaming for help, and people were watching, but none of them was doing anything to help. He forced her into an alley between two shops, and her cries rang out into the street.

'Fuck! Did you see that?' I said, startled.

215

Ben nodded grimly. The lights changed and the car moved forward. But then Ben braked suddenly and snapped out of his seat-belt.

'Can't have that,' he said, more to himself than to me.

'Ben, he had a knife!' I yelled, as he opened the car door and leapt out. While I fumbled with my seat-belt, I saw Ben race across the road, into the alley. The engine was still running, and Kate Bush kept singing. While I was staggering out of the car, I heard more angry shouts. There was a silence, then the woman started screaming again. Next, a man leapt out of the alley and fled down the street at an incredible pace, and the man who was running wasn't my brother. It wasn't Ben.

Instantly, I sobered up. Shaking with panic, I ran across the road. I was almost hit by a taxi, which braked just in time, its bumper swelling forward, gently nuzzling my legs and knocking me off balance.

He was lying on his side in a pile of trash. Blood was pouring from a huge knife wound in his neck. He looked dazed, as if he was desperately trying to remember something. The woman who'd been attacked wasn't there. I hadn't passed her in the street, and the alley led only to a padlocked door in a high brick wall. Yet she was nowhere to be seen.

I tried to press my right hand over the long wedgeshaped gash in my brother's neck. Now that the danger had passed, people passing by came forward to offer help. An old black guy in a flat cap took off his jacket and laid it over Ben's legs. Someone else went off to phone for an ambulance. A group of silent teenagers stood around to watch.

Ben's face had turned the colour and texture of ivory. The man in the flat cap knelt down beside me to offer encouragement. 'Keep on holding him, man. Keep on holding him.'

Ben was trying to say something. 'Will there . . .'

'Shh,' I said.

'Will there be . . .'

'Shush, Ben,' I said. 'Try not to talk.'

(*Will there be cars there? Tattoos and muscles? Will there be jobs that can't be explained? Will there be Sam Cook, a freeway to drive down? Will there be toothbrushes? Will there be love?*)

The Secret Sexist

It seems such an irony, now. On the same night that I, sensible trustworthy Guy, owner of five A levels and a cycling proficiency certificate, was almost arrested for using a loud-hailer to insult a man with undersized genitals, Ben, my violent and educationally subnormal brother, voted the son least likely to succeed by his own parents, lost his life while trying to protect a woman from an assault at knife point.

Ben might have lived, had the ambulance not taken twenty-five minutes to arrive. He got his face on the front cover of the *Manchester Evening News*. The headline read 'Ambulance Tragedy of Knife-Attack Hero'. Questions were asked in the House of Commons, and the Health Secretary said, in the government's defence, that there were more ambulances than at any time in the history of the Health Service, but forgot to mention that there was no one to fucking drive them.

I felt like a liar, telling the police that Ben had been stabbed trying to save a vanished woman from a vanished attacker. Yet the two officers who interviewed me accepted my version of events without question. The amount of shaking and crying I was doing might have had something to do with it. I helped a police artist to assemble a photofit of Ben's killer. By the time I'd finished, half the Greater Manchester police were out searching for Bluto from the Popeye cartoons.

I knew that this was my chance to finally grow up and

repay Ben for the support he'd lent me when Gina had died. Or at least, to repay his widow and his children on his behalf, by making any arrangements that were necessary. That, I know, would have been the manly thing to do.

But I cannot be a man, my friend, because I simply caved in. Within five months, I'd lost two people whom I adored, and I didn't feel I had the courage or the energy to face the world any more. I went back to my room in Natalie's house, drew the curtains, climbed into bed and gave up.

Natalie, white as a ghost, held my hand as I lay there. All her coldness had melted away. She tried to talk to me. But I would not, could not answer. She laid Erik on the pillow beside me. I suppose she thought that the sight of him would give me hope or something. But the baby's smile reminded me of Gina, and his bad haircut reminded me of Ben, and I couldn't bear to look at him.

Then something extraordinary happened. Natalie's friends, the three separatists who had refused to enter her house as long as I lived there, broke their vows. They came in through the front door, their arms laden with food and flowers. They answered the phone, cooked, cleaned and looked after the baby, while Natalie did what she could to help Rachel.

For a whole week, Les and Amanda and Freddy lived in the same house as a man who had offended them. But not Anne Fermesky. Anne Fermesky did not come. If you want miracles, read the bible.

Les Bean served me delicious nutritious meals which I couldn't eat. With grace and patience, two or three times a day, she carried food in to me and then returned to carry it away, untasted. Sometimes she smiled at me, even though she knew that I possessed a penis which, on occasion, had been known to grow erect.

On the seventh morning, Amanda came into the room to pin something to Gina's shrine.

'What's that?' I asked her. I thought it would probably be a poster that read 'All Men are Guilty of Rape'.

She turned to smile at me. 'It's a photo of your brother.'

It was a snap I'd taken last summer, while Ben had been hitting his car with a spanner, something that he liked to do every weekend. He was grinning directly at the camera, black grease all over his face, looking like young Burt Reynolds when he needed a bath. It was a nice picture.

Later that day Natalie came in to inform me that the police were treating Ben's death as murder. This meant that his body was being retained as evidence, and that his funeral would be delayed indefinitely. 'So,' she said, demonstrating her customary insight, 'you needn't feel bad because you haven't done enough. Rachel's need isn't going to go away. She needs us now, and she'll need us when Ben's buried. There's still a lot we can do.'

I nodded. She gave my nose a tweak. 'Now, will you please eat something? Because I happen to like you and you're getting rather thin.'

She brought in some lentil soup, home-made by Les, and proceeded to spoon-feed me. I was perfectly capable of feeding myself, but it was more fun to be fed by Natalie. After she'd wiped my mouth on a napkin, I said, 'Where are the women?'

'They've gone,' she said. 'They know the worst is over, now.'

'How do they know that?'

'Because women understand these things,' she said.

'What things? What the fuck are you talking about?'

She didn't reply. 'I'm going to run you a bath, and I'll even wash your hair for you. If you want me to.'

Being bathed by Natalie was not as erotic as I might have hoped. Misery and self-inflicted starvation had made me frail and weak, like an old, old man. My head throbbed, and my bones ached. My legs and chest had grown pitifully thin, and, judging by the smell, rats had been nesting in my armpits.

Natalie dried me with a huge fleecy bath towel, gently, as if I were a priceless antique. I couldn't stop crying. She left me to blubber while she changed my sheets. Then I climbed into bed and sank into a deep, exhausted sleep.

'When do you want me to go?'

It was the evening of the following day, and I'd finally arisen, showered and dressed. We were in the conservatory. Erik wouldn't go to sleep, so we'd laid him on a mat between us. He was naked, waggling his legs as he sucked a teddy bear's ear. The windows to the garden were open. Dusk was falling. The buttercups were catching fire in the deep grass.

Natalie looked at me intently. 'What d'you mean?'

'You know . . . when do you want me to leave?'

'Oh, that's all changed,' she announced. 'You're staying here with me, now.'

'But I failed all six tasks.'

'Six tasks? Why? What was the sixth?'

'You know – the way you tested me by sleeping with Mitchell.'

'Guy, I never slept with Mitchell.'

'But I saw him in our bathroom, with his spotty cock and his horrible ginger arse.'

Amusement filled her face. 'He stopped round for a shower after playing a charity football match.'

'You never slept with him?'

'No. And I never would.'

'So after failing the five tasks, I failed a task that wasn't even a task?'

She nodded and laughed. 'Pretty good going, eh? But none of that matters now. It isn't important.'

221

'Am I still a sexist bastard?'

'Yep.'

'Thanks.' Resentfully, I added, 'I didn't fail all the tasks, you know.'

She smiled apologetically. 'The tasks meant nothing. They were a joke. Your friends were right, Guy. Didn't you realize? It was something me and the sisters dreamed up. We were having a fucking good laugh at your expense. It was obvious how badly you wanted to screw me. We were curious to see what lengths you were prepared to go to in order to achieve your aim.'

Crushed, I said, 'And now you know.'

'I'm sorry.'

'No. No, it was very witty,' I admitted. 'You really had me by the balls, there.'

With a trace of regret, she said, 'Yeah. But it was nasty, too. 'Cause while we were having fun, putting this dumb chauvinist through his paces, none of us believed that you were proving anything, or were even *worth* anything. By your own admission, you'd danced around this house with my knickers on your head. You could have raised millions of pounds for cancer research, and it would have made no difference. We'd still have thought of you as an ignorant slob who'd go to any extremes to get his end away.'

'Not any extremes. I'd never have put Anne Fermesky's knickers on my head.' I sighed, realizing what a fool I'd been. 'But why, Nat? What made you want to do that to me?'

She left her chair and crouched beside Erik. Then she pressed her right thumb into his left hand and watched as his tiny fingers closed around it. When she turned to look at me, her eyes were full of pain. 'You betrayed Gina. I really hated you for that.'

I must have looked hurt, because she picked the baby up and placed him in my lap. 'Come on,' she said. 'Come and see your daddy.'

Gingerly, I placed my arm behind Erik's neck to support his head. 'Where's his nappy? What if he shits on me?'

'It'll serve you right.'

'Do you still hate me?'

She knelt beside me and slipped her hand into mine. 'Hey. Come on ... None of that matters, now. Not after what's happened.'

'Oh, great. Fine. It doesn't matter, but I'm still a sexist bastard.'

'Yes, you are. So am I. So's *everyone*. But we're intelligent people. Between us, I'm sure we can work something out.'

'Like what, exactly?'

She gave me one of those long, slow Natalie stares. 'Let's try something out. Call it an experiment ... let's forget everything we've been taught and start again.'

I laughed. 'What? Like Adam and Eve?'

'No, because Adam and Eve knew they were man and woman. Let's forget about gender too. Let's just be people.'

'What do people do?'

'I don't know,' she said, squeezing my hand. 'Let's find out.'